Ask **Hayley,** Ask **Justin**

Justin Lookadoo is the original "humoticator™," meaning he uses humor to motivate and educate teens. He is considered *the* speaker for the ADD Generation, training kids in spirituality and success. He has worked with over 300,000 young people and is in demand both nationally and internationally for radio, TV, and personal appearances. He ignites in teens a passion to design their lives and live with purpose, not as spectators but as the stars.
Visit www.lookadoo.com for more info.

Ask Justin

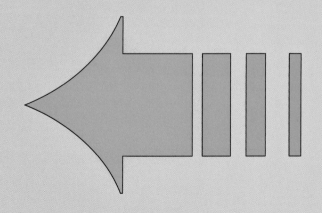

Posted by: 34Redbirde

My friends say that extasy is a safe drug. Does that mean that it's ok for me to take it?

Dear Redbirde,

Just because something is safe doesn't make it right. Safe sex isn't any more holy than unsafe sex. So safety isn't the question. The question is about control. If you've seen people on extasy you see how they behave. They tend to be very touchy and sexual, very spacey and dazed. They have no hindrances any longer, they would be very easy to take advantage of. They only want to be satisfied. Taking drugs is always about feeling good. It's always self-absorbed. It's just about making you feel good. God wants us to be alert to what others need. He wants us to be aware of our surroundings so we won't sin, and when you are high you have little concept of the sin you are acting out. If you want to live according to God's plan then extasy is not the way to go, even if it's completely safe.

Subj: Repentance

Clive,

Dude, repentance isn't about crying and getting all emotional. Saying "I'm sorry" isn't even the deal. In fact, who cares if you believe what you did was wrong if you don't stop doing it? Man, to repent all you gotta do is STOP DOING IT. But check this, when you repent, it doesn't mean you are suddenly perfect. It just means you're doing what God said to do today. So don't get all teary-eyed just get over it and get on with life.

Check out Matthew 27:3, Matthew 9:13, Luke 5:32 and Genesis 6:6-7

Ask **Justin**

3

Posted by: Tom3

I have been gay a long time, ever sense I was like six or something. I was raped back then, now I'm all messed up. I go on all these nasty sites; my cousin (who raped me) always comes over and tries things with me, and today he came over and we did some things that we shouldn't have. I don't understand. It's crazy cause I have been doing this for years, and it seems I can't shake it. I mean I know the LORD wants me to be free too, but I don't think he is showing me a way to get out of all this. I'm tired. I'd love any help you could offer, thanks.

Tom3,

Forget what happened when you were six; it sucks, but your life is now, and you can only change what's now. When God saves us He never tells us things are going to get easy, no matter who we are. Staying pure is just as hard for straight people as it is for gay people. Your sexual desire isn't the issue as much as your giving into it is. Being tempted is not sin, but acting out on it or even considering it is. Jesus was tempted and did not sin. So don't think God has forsaken you just 'cuz you are still tempted.

You have to learn how to control your thoughts so that they don't go where they shouldn't. When you start to think impure thoughts stop them immediately and think about something else, anything else.

Here are some more things to do:

- → Quit hanging out with your cousin alone.
- → Do not participate in homosexual activity.
- → Get all porn out of your room and life. Get a porn blocker for the Internet, trash all your mags and movies.
- → Stay away from anything that makes you think about sex—TV shows, DVDs, songs, etc.
- → Stay away from danger zones. If alone in your bedroom is a danger zone, get out. Usually danger zones are isolated places.

What to do when the urge takes control.

- → Get around people. Go into the living room. Go to the store. Whatever. The crowd will assure that you will not fall into the pressure.
- → Get on the phone with someone. (Not IM or web chat.) A real person.
- → Keep your mind busy. Do something you enjoy to keep your thoughts off sex. Read. Pray. Do Homework. Play Nintendo.

This will be tough but you can do it. You are in control. This did not become a habit overnight and you cannot change it overnight. But be strong. Stick to it. This will work and you will win.

Posted by: Tempted
I'm a 17-year-old male and I have a g/f. We are tempted to have sex, and I was wondering if we do will we be forgiven afterwards??

Tempted,

Duh! Who isn't tempted to have sex? But your real question is about forgiveness not sex. What you are really asking is if I walked up and spit in your face and rub dirt all in it but I am going to say "I'm sorry" will that be OK. No it's not OK! That's stupid.

Deal with the real issue. Take control of this area of your life and you will see other areas where you will gain control. God wants to give you all your dreams, but there is a deal to be made, and your end of the deal is that you are faithful.

I promise you, save the sex for the marriage and you will have the best sex you could ever dream of. Compromise and take a little piece of it today and watch your marriage lose its passion later on. Also, don't forget the fact that having a baby at age 17 sucks. And it is very, very easy to get her pregnant. No contraceptive works 100% of the time. Don't buy the lie. Keep the faith and your entire life will be a success.

Posted by: Ashamed
I'm sexually addicted. I forget what it's called,
"mastublating," or something like that. It means getting
the pleasure of sex, only by yourself. I've even thought of
hitting on girls that I know. I'm 12. I'm too young for this.

Dear Ashamed,
Check out what I told Tom3 on pg. 4. The same deal will
work for you too.

Justin

7

Posted by: D.J.

I am having a hard time with it I really don't know how to tell my friends without them running away

Dear D.J.

Let's go over what a friend isn't. A friend isn't someone who takes a hike just because you don't agree with them. And they don't get all over you because of who you are. Man, a friend is someone who totally digs you even if they don't get you. If these dorks are truly your friends they won't run away just cuz of what your Dad does. Give 'em some credit. They can't be so shallow that they can't handle a pastor's kid.

Posted by: really mature

I am a twenty-one year old guy. I have been living on my own since I was sixteen. A lot of my non-Christian friends are saying that I act too old and that I need to enjoy my youth. I want to, but I want to give my youth to Jesus. But I don't know where to start. My friends are right. I act too old. Should I be trying to enjoy the time I have left as a young adult or just plunge in to adulthood and ignore them?

Dear Really Mature,

Dude, if you are holding back on life because you think God wants you to be boring you are wrong. Christ said He came to give us life to the full. That means full of laughter, pain, heartache, joy. All kinds of stuff. Don't think you have to hold back because you gotta be an adult. Be yourself. Be the man He made. And live life to the full.

Subj: no friends

Posted by: Wowme

I'm not asking to be super popular but I would like a few people to like me and be a faithful friend to me. Also, I am scared to walk into rooms with people in them. I am always self-conscious. How can I be confident? How can I make others like me and want to be around me. I am very sad.

Dear Wowme,

OK, it's time to renew your mind. Stop spending so much time looking at all the negatives. We're supposed to think about stuff that's cool, awesome, exciting and all that good stuff (Phillipians 4). You have to take the negative thinking out of your head. Try this, whenever you start to think these stupid thoughts say 'No,' literally say *no*, and start thinking about something good. Change the cycle. Renew your mind cuz you are not living a life of faith right now. You're a kid of a king. You should be the most confident person in the room.

Dear Giggles,

It's like this Giggles. The way you dress influences the way you are treated. If you dress modestly, you will be treated like you are valuable and have important, interesting stuff inside you. If you dress like Britney Spears, you will not get treated like a superstar, you will get treated like a tramp. Why? Because you are showing your business. Guys won't ever see *you*. They won't be able to get past the flesh you're flaunting. So think about it. Decide how do you want to be treated and dress to fit that.

Posted by: X-tremeGuro1
Sometimes I feel that there is just so much pressure and I don't know what to do? I go to public school and am made fun of because my looks and beliefs. I am a Christian. I know God says to "stick up for you beliefs" but sometimes its tuff. What do I do?

Dear X-tremeGuro1,

Try being a contagious Christian. Figure out how to be so appealing to everyone that they want to know you and not dis' you. Get really good at loving people. How? Learn to care about them, not preach at them. Get artistic, people love artistic people. Ask questions about their lives and don't judge their responses. Remember, it's not your job to fix 'em, just to show 'em God's love. Laugh a lot. Laughing draws people together. You don't have to be a geek to be a Christian. You can draw more people to Christ by caring about them then by fearing them. Your job isn't to stick up for yourself, your job is to show them Christ. And remember, Christ was never offended for himself only for His Father. A change in attitude on your part might be just what the world needs in order to see Christ in you.

Dear Amanda,

Tell her that whatever she can't overcome will become her identity. Yeah, it sucks that she was abused, but if she doesn't get over it all she will be her entire life is an abused little kid. The way she does this is by forgiveness. She has to forgive her uncle, even if he doesn't deserve it. Then she has to get on with her life. She has forgiven him, God has cleansed her. She is a new creation and needs to act and think like it. God makes all things new.

   2 Corinthians 1:3–4; Psalm 40:1–3; 116:5–7; Isaiah 41:13; 57:18

Posted by: GuyforGod
Ok, how come I can drink wine in church, but I can't drink it anywhere else?

GuyforGod –

Cuz it's against the law! Dude, in church it's ok cuz it's part of communion. It's part of the service. You know that as soon as you get outside church and start drinking your gonna want more than a thimble full. Listen, drinking isn't a sin, but getting drunk is. And when you are a kid getting drunk is really tempting. So obey your parents and lay off, you will all be happier.

Check out Scripture for more stuff on drinking: Prov. 13:15;14:18;20:1;31:4-5; 1 Corinthians 10:23-33

Posted by: 4him53

My Dad drinks like three or four beers every night. Is that a sin? How much can you drink before it is a sin?

Dear 4him53 –

1.5 cups.

Wouldn't you love it if I could tell you that easily. There is no easy answer. Drinking alcohol is not a sin in Scripture. Heck, even Jesus turned water into alcohol at a party. But getting drunk is a different story.

I can't tell you if your Dad is drunk. And frankly, there is nothing you can do about his drinking anyway. So don't worry about his sin. Pray for him. Let God take care of what you can't.

Posted by: Matt

My brother says he has a guardian angel watching over him. Is that weird, like some kind of imaginary friend or something?

Matt –

If he starts talking to him and introducing him at parties it might be a little weird. But Psalms says we each have an angle protecting us, so he's right. Nothin freaky here.

Check out Psalm 91:11-12.

Posted by: Lonely
My parents aren't Christians and they think that my faith is stupid. They smoke pot a lot and want me to smoke with them. I know I am supposed to honor my parents, but I'm also not supposed to break the law. What do I do?

Dear Lonely –
Dang, that's tough. Why not send in an anonymous tip to the police about your parents drugs. They need to get clean. No, you don't honor your parents by breaking God's law. God comes first, then your parents. So whatever they tell you to do that is against Him, you don't do.

Posted by: Jim
I got really mad at my sister yesterday. Does that mean I'm not a Christian?

Dear Jim –
No. It means you *are* human.

Posted by: Clark

My Dad kicks my dog when he's mad. Is it a sin to be mean like that to animals?

Dear Clark,

So not cool! Dad's got issues. We are put on the earth to care for it. Even animals. It is sinful to disregard this command. Try talking to your dad about treating your dog better, or mention it to your mom. You've got a responsibility to make sure the dog is treated right just like your dad does.

Check out Proverbs 12:10.

Posted by: cool*guy

A couple of my friends dyed their hair green. Is it ok if I dye my hair or is God against that?

Dear Cool*Guy,

Why? You gotta be like everyone else or something? Can't you come up with something original? Dying your hair is not listed in the Bible as a sin, but my question is still why? Is it a God thing, a fun thing or a 'I gotta fit in' thing?

Posted by: FlipperZ
My Mom says I can't get a tattoo because it's wrong she says.
Where is that in the Bible?

Dear FlipperZ –

Don't argue with your mom. That said, here is what she's
talking about. Leviticus 19:28, you ready? "You shall not . . .
tattoo any marks on you: I am the Lord." Gulp! Bet you didn't
know that was there, huh? Ok, I know, it's Old Testament,
what does that have to do with us. Good question, cuz for
some things Christ came to relieve us of slavery to the law.
Is this one of them? Maybe. Tats aren't the issue. The issue
is that your parents don't want you to do it. And that is a no
brainer, obey your parents, it's a commandment.

About the tattoo though. It's not that big a deal when we
are talking about sin and Jesus and stuff. But consider that
your body is the temple of God. Do you want graffiti all over
it? What will you do when you are a wrinkled old man
trying to hide all the marks?

Subj: Church

Posted by: Alex 78

My friend says he's a Christian but he goes to church on Saturdays, aren't we supposed to go on the Sabbath, Sunday? Does God care what day you do church?

Dear Alex,

No. He just wants you to go to church. Monday, Tuesday, Wednesday, whenever. Do you know when the Sabbath really is? It's on Saturday. But after Jesus came the Sabbath was changed to Sunday, the day He was resurrected.

The Sabbath is a day set aside when all you do is worship God, hang out with Him, pray to Him and think about Him. It's all God, all day. So pick the day that's best for you and honor Him on it. That's the most important thing.

'Remember the Sabbath and keep it holy." Exodus 20:8

Justin

Posted by: Cliffclimber1
If God made pot, why can't I smoke it?

Dear Cliffclimber–

Cuz it's illegal! God made dogs poop too, does that mean you should eat it? Stupid logic dude. It's against the law, so stay away from it.

The Bible says that everything is permissible but not everything is beneficial. Pot was made by God and some people say that's a reason to smoke it. But God made lots of poisonous plants, should we smoke those too? The trouble with pot is this:

→ It is illegal, and gotta obey the law.
→ It controls you. Pot makes people act stupid.
→ It's bad for your health. It kills brain cells.

So yes, God made pot, but he also made poison ivy, you gonna smoke that too?

Posted by: Tiff

I have a lil' question. I know that sex isn't at all in the plan of things till marriage . . . nor am I even pondering that. But I was wondering, is even a little kiss wrong. I know some may say that a kiss can lead onto bigger things . . . I believe that, but isn't a little smooch o.k??? Yet, this guy . . . we're good friends, and I'm talkin' to him about God too, every time I've gotten near him lately it's like "I wanna share my 1st kiss with him"

I just wanted to know if a kiss was ok to God???

Tiff,

Check out what I told Matt who asked How Far is Too Far? It's not about rules, it's about your motives. What are you trying to get out of this? Are you obsessed with the idea of kissing this guy? Pray about this. Sit there and imagine Jesus with you on a date with the guy. Would you kiss him? Would you still want to kiss him?

Posted by: Brett

My best friend fasts all the time. She says he is doing it because she wants to get close to God but I think she's doing it to lose weight. What can I do?

Dear Brett –

Your friend has issues. Killing yourself and pretending like it's all for God is mixed up.

Fasting is cool when God calls you to it. But if she's doing it all the time it's probably anorexia. Help her get counseling. Anorexics don't know when they are anorexic, so friends have to help point it out.

Posted by: Josh

I get porno on my computer EVERY day! Is there anything that I can do? I don't want Satan's trash in my box and I'm scared becuz he is so sneaky and I'm scared my mom will find it and think I am a nasty kid. Isn't this illegal? I am 14.

Dear Josh,

Unfortunately, there is no way to get rid of all that junk mail that comes into your account. There are some service providers that can block some of it but not all. If I were you I'd give your parents a heads up. Tell them you get it but you don't want to. Ask if they can help block it. Their mission is to help teens with internet porn.

Remember, keep accountability partners. Delete anything suspicious before you open it. It's a battle, but you CAN fight it and win.

Posted by: beck

I have to choose which parent to move in with and it is hard for me to do. I want to stay here with my dad but I don't want to be in yelling and screaming everyday but I will still be in a church. And I want to with my mom because she cares for me more and so does the guy she is seeing. Please reply to this because I will get really upset and will give up on God again and will try to hurt myself.

Dear Beck,

Dude what's with the "I will get really upset and will give up on God again and will try to hurt myself" dang? You have manipulation issues kicking. Deal with those. Be yourself and just be straight up and ask for help.

As far as where you move? If your mom is cool with you hooking up with a church and growing, go there. The yelling and screaming every day will totally beat you down. Get to a place that is encouraging and safe.

Posted by: Alan
If someone does not believe in God, can he not declare himself a god? If someone finds themselves feeling helpless and unhelped because they cannot see God in their lives, wouldn't it be beneficial for that person to find some way to empower themselves?

Dear Alan,

First, I can declare myself a bulldozer all day long. But it ain't happening. Someone can declare themselves a god . . . it ain't happening. If someone is searching enough to try to empower themselves, they NEED God. Just because someone doesn't see Him working doesn't mean he's not real. They would be much better off if they "declared" themselves a full on follow of Jesus the Christ.

Posted by: Scott

Why is a religion, the set of rules, tradition and ritual, necessary if you have an individual faith in God that you feel content with?

Dear Scott,

Religion is not necessary. That's like saying why are the rules, traditions and rituals necessary to play basketball. They're not. But it helps the gave move smoother and faster and it gives you a guide. That is like with the whole religion thing. It help give you some direction on how to create a deep relationship with God the Father without getting majorly sidetracked.

Posted by: Todd

What is God and the modern church's view on homosexuality and its place in our world?

Dear Todd,

You want God's view, or the modern church's? Start with God. Rom. 1 says that it is impurity. It's a sin, just like gossiping about your g/f is a sin. That doesn't mean that you are going to hell, it just means you need to stop acting on your impulses.

The modern church's view can be a little more harsh. Many people in the church see it like the worst of all evils. They freak out on it as if it's worse than murder or something. But they are looking at it through human eyes. God says, it's a sin. It's not how I made you, so stop.

Posted by: Rick

I am a little unsure of what, specifically, the Original Sin was and why we should feel accountable.

Dear Rick,

The original sin isn't one specific sin. It means that when you're born, you're sinful. You need God.

Posted by: Dragon

I have had a lot of trouble lately. I am a born Catholic but I don't exactly agree with everything that we are supposed to believe. What am I supposed to do? I am so lost.

Dear Dragon,

First of all you aren't born anything but a baby. You have to make a decision once you are older about what God you will follow. Sounds like you just need to do a little research. Start reading the Bible. Get a version you can understand. Find out what God wants from you. Then see how that matches what the church wants from you. Talk to a priest. Get the facts and then go with what God is telling you to do.

I was just wondering is MTV or rap music bad to watch and listen to?

Dear 4-Christ,

I see God in some major ways on MTV. But, I don't feed my mind that stuff 24/7. Whatever you constantly feed your mind, that is what you will believe. So spend more time talking to God and reading the Word. Dig into that and then you will see Him everywhere.

Posted by: Wondering

Everyone at school hates me. What should I do?

Dear wondering,

No. Everyone does not hate you. You can't possibly know what every person is thinking. Stop being so emotional about it and start trying to be fun to be with. Maybe you are just quiet, or shy or boring. They just might not know you. Try to come out of your shell. Try art, try music. Read the paper. Make conversation. They will start to see who you are and start acting more like friends.

Posted by: Ethan

What do you think, as teenagers, that the age gap between members of an intimate relationship (like boyfriend/girlfriend) should be? One year? two? three? Could, for example, a 14-year-old "go out" with a 19-year-old?

Ethan,

Adolescence is one of the times bodies and emotions develop the fastest, so a 19 and 14 dating is a lot different from a 25 and 30 dating.

There is something really weird about a 19-year-old wanting to go out with a 14-year-old. The 19-year-old has issues. If you're noticing a hot 14-year-old right now, think back to how you acted when you were that age. She may seem mature, but she's still 14. Don't get into something for looks anyway, make sure there's real friendship there.

Stick with relationships close to your own age. But also know that at 14 years old, that relationship will not last forever. So don't get all wrapped up in them. Take it easy.

Posted by: Matt

My question is simple to me but complicated to everyone I ask? My girlfriend and I are both Christians and have decided to become ministers in the future. The problem were having is how far is too far to go? We have never had sex and were waiting till were married. Please help.

Matt,

The question is not so simple. What you are wanting is someone to give you permission to do things. But, here. Would you be embarrassed to tell your mom, your little sister, your grandma, or even your pastor what you did? If you would be, don't do it.

Even with kissing. Can you imagine the audience with your pastor and fam and her pastor and fam and telling them all the details. I kissed her on the lips. I nibbled on her neck. I stuck my tongue in her mouth. I sucked on her lip. Yeah, granny would love that.

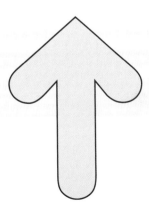

I have been wandering lately what a girl should dress like? What I mean is how baggy do the clothes have to be? Please tell me exactly what hinders you when you see a girl wearing something. I want to help you guys out by not wearing inappropriate clothing. Please do not hold back on your answers.

Polly,

Here's a little trip inside a guy's mind:

→ Short shorts or short skirts: we are staring at your legs trying to see your butt.

→ Spaghetti straps or low cut stuff: we are trying to look down your shirt

→ Super tight clothes: we are staring at every curve

→ Showing your stomach: we are just groping all over it

Subj: masturbation

Posted by: evan

Is it okay to masturbate . . . what does the Bible say? Do you have to lust when you masturbate or can it be just a physical thing to get rid of the sexual tensions?

Dear Evan,

The Bible doesn't say anything specifically about it.

The question is what's running in your mind. If you're imagining women or sex, then you're sinning. But, because it puts you in an altered state it can be addictive. I'd avoid it. Go running, work out, think about something different.

Subj: girls

Posted by: Luke
I wanna know is it okay to go out with a non-believer?

Luke–

No. You will get emotionally involved and influenced by someone who is not listening to God. Also, you are trying to walk closer and closer to knowing God. That is not the direction they are walking so to stay together, you will have to stop running after God.

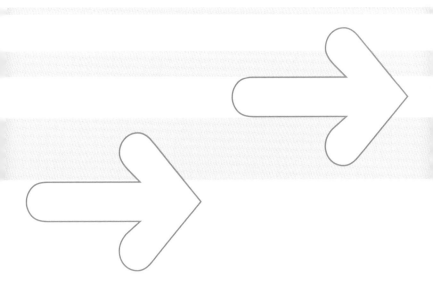

What is going to happen or what will we do up there? Will there be anymore hurting, pain, tears, crying & anything else that is going on here on earth?

Hey William,

Check out Revelation 21:10–27. It's a really great image of heaven. There are huge walls that look like diamonds. The gates to the wall are giant pearls. The streets are paved with gold. It's totally gorgeous. It's all the absolute best moments in your life put together; no—it's better than that. Billy Graham's daughter, Anne Graham Lotz, recently wrote a book on heaven called *In My Father's House*. You can read that or listen to the tape to find out more of what heaven will be like.

Posted by: john
Sometimes in church some people start to speak in tongues and since I can't understand it I start to get annoyed and think it is stupid. Can any body help me?????

John,

Hard one for me too. I am way open to anything. But when people get into the tongues and stuff, my first reaction is like yours . . . shut up. But, I learned that hey, that's just not my deal. I don't have to understand it. And I don't have to do it. I finally quit thinking about them as posers and fakes and doing it because other people are. It's not my job to judge them. So now, I love it. It's cool to watch and experience. It's still not my deal. And I am OK with that. God and I do our thing a little different than them. Neither is right and it's all good.

1 Corinthians 14

Posted by: frustrated

Why when you ask a non-Christian what they did last weekend they're not ashamed to tell you if they smoked pot, had sex with their girlfriend or boyfriend, or even robbed a bank. But when you ask a Christian, a lot of the time they are ashamed to tell you if you had an awesome God encounter, went to an awesome worship service, or witnessed to their friend?

Dear Frustrated,

People screw up sometimes. They don't always act the way they should. The Bible does make it clear that we should not be embarrassed of our relationship with God. And don't let culture influence you—get out there and do what you know is right.

Posted by: PrettyGirl

I am about 100 pounds heavier than my friends. I am a good student, a good friend and pretty too I think, except for all of the weight. My question is: Seriously. Would you date a fat girl? What about a SUPER FAT GIRL like me? What about marriage? Would it embarrass you to have a fat wife?

Dear PrettyGirl,

Hate to say it, but guys are into looks. Now, I am not saying you have to have a perfect bod, but you gotta look like you take care of yourself. Being hugely overweight is less about the way you look and more about what that says. The message it sends is that you don't take care of yourself and you have no self-control.

Yes, God looks at the inside and knows your heart. But you asked about people's reactions. Again, I am not saying you have to be a 125 lb. girl. Not at all. But you do need to take care of your body.

Don't worry about your future though. God's got plans for you and if that involves a husband, he'll love you no matter what you look like.

Posted by: Micah

How do you use the name of the Lord in vain? Is it wrong to say "God!" or "Oh my Lord!"

Micah,

Yeah, all the usual things about God's name apply. But this biggest way I see people using the Lord's name in vain is putting it all over every billboard, business card and bumper sticker. Hey, if you are a good plumber, be the best plumber in town. You'll get the business. Don't try to get the Christian sympathy business by putting a cross on you business card. And W.W.J.D? He wouldn't wear a bracelet around asking the question. He'd be living his life so that you wouldn't have to advertise it. So I think there are a lot more not cool ways of using the name of our Savior in vain.

Subj: calling

Posted by: Taylor
Why do you think men should call girls or whatever? I don't understand that, you mean you think men should pursue women??

Taylor,

Get a grip on the truth. Guys love a challenge. It comes from cave man days of chasing down the Lunchasourus and clubbing him in the head. We love the chase. The game. When a girl starts asking us out, yeah we like it. It strokes our ego. But, WE WILL GET BORED! And when that happens . . . next. So guys need to step up and be the man. And let the girl be the woman. Ug!

Ask Both of Us

Posted by: trina29

What do you think about b/f's tickling their g/f's?

Dear Trina,

The real deal is not what do I think about it, but why are you doing what you are doing? It is a motive question. What are your motives? When you do it do you hope he will touch you more or his hand will slip? If you or he have sexual thoughts about it, then it's probably not a good thing to be doing. Check what you are thinking. Where do you want it to lead? Everything you do is taking you somewhere. Where is tickling taking you?

Hayley

Trina,

Tickling = Foreplay.

That is straight from a guy's perspective. It is sexual. Girls can call it flirting, playing or whatever. For guys, we just want to be able to touch your body. And he is going to let his hands tickle you everywhere he can touch. Because "Hey, we were just playing. It was no big deal." And there is no such thing as a guy letting his hands "slip." He always knows where they are and puts them where he wants them . . . uh . . . I mean accidentally. So don't do it. It's doing nothing good.

Justin

Read Philippians 4:8–9 for more help.

Posted by: Sherri
My friend only uses laxatives or throws up only once in a while, like if she wants to lose 5 pounds for a date. That's not so bad, is it?

Dear Sherri,
Your friend probably has a problem with bulimia. She might not be telling you everything, but even if she is, this is dangerous behavior. Obviously her body is something she feels like she can control with violence. Forcing yourself to throw up is an attack against your body. It is not healthy and is incredibly destructive.

You need to tell an adult who can help her, like her mom, a counselor, a teacher, a pastor. She will probably be really mad at you, but would you rather have her mad or dead? If you love your friend you will find a way to get her some help before she kills herself.

Hayley

Sherri
Yeah, your friend has got issues. Especially if she is barfin' for a guy. The guy WON'T EVEN NOTICE! Definitely needs help.

Justin

Look at what the Bible has to say about this: 1 Corinthians 3:16–17, 1 Corinthians 6:19–20.

Posted by: Kim4Christ

I have a friend whose boyfriend just broke up with her after almost a year. She is really heart-broken and really wants them to get back together. This has never happened to me, so what should I say to her that will help her get over him? I know that I should be there for her as a friend and hug her and love her, but how can she get over him?

Dear Kim,

The answer is time. There is no way to hurry up and get over someone. It really hurts and it takes time for the pain to go away. The best counsel is Scripture. Search it out and find passages that talk about trusting God with our lives. That's what she is being tested with right now. Will she trust God to work all things out for good, or will she fail the test and take everything into her own hands? There is something bigger than this relationship with the ex, and that is her relationship with God. What will she do now? Worship the old relationship or her God?

Hayley

Kim,

Your friend needs to realize that the relationship will not last. Period. So why pour everything into a relationship that will not last? If she goes back to the guy telling him how much she wants him back, yeah, he may do it, because it's an ego trip for the guy. It made him feel good. Once that is gone, say buh-bye to the relationship again. Walk away. If you want to know the real deal on relationships then check out my book called *Dateable*.

Justin

"My grace is sufficient for you, for my power is made perfect in weakness . . . That is why, for Christ's sake, I delight in weaknesses, in insults, in hardship, in persecution, in difficulties. For when I am weak, then I am strong" (2 Corinthians 12:9–10).

Subj: "Going out"

Posted by: Petite Princess
I was just wondering—what exactly does it mean when somebody says they're "going out" with somebody? What does "going out" involve? For somebody my age (14), I mean.

Dear Petite Princess,

That's a good question. Going out comes from the idea that two people go somewhere together. And when they go places together a lot they say that they are "going out." But, depending on your age it could mean all different things. If you are in middle school and don't drive yet, then going out means that a boy and girl like each other. This might mean that they talk to each other at lunch, know each other's locker combination and tell everyone they are going out. It just kind of lets the world know that you both think the other person is cute.

As you get older, things get a little more serious. Boys and girls that are going out will hold hands, study together, talk a lot on the phone, stuff like that.

When you get to high school and are driving, going out literally means going out and doing things together. Going to the movies, dinner, miniature golfing, stuff like that. And at that age it probably means that you are committed to liking only each other. That's when all that messy break up stuff starts to happen.

Hayley

Petite Princess,

I don't have a clue. Going out. Dating. Seeing each other. Hanging out. Hooking up. I always just ask whoever says it, "What do you mean when you say that?" Cuz the answer is always different. I think the most accurate title would be "going together." Because for the most part, that is what you are doing. You go to the dance together. You go to school together. You go to the movie together. Hey, you are just going together.

Justin

Check this out: Matthew 6:33–34.

Posted by: PurpleSoul

I am a fourteen yr. old teen who has a question... Is it bad for me to have a boyfriend right now at my age??? Is there anything in the Bible about when it's ok to date? Please help. I need to know.

Dear PurpleSoul,

There is not one mention of dating in the Bible. Dating is a fairly new idea. In biblical times people didn't marry based on who was cute, smartest or sexiest. They married based on who God called them to marry, usually through the arrangement of their parents. Dating today has more to do with satisfying our earthly desires than it does with serving God.

No, it's not wrong for you to date if you are looking for a husband. You have to know a person before you marry them and dating is one way to do that. But I would bet that at 14 you are not ready to be married. So my suggestion would be put off the dating stuff 'til you are ready for what it leads to, marriage. Just have friends, hang out, but don't commit to anyone yet, and don't get physical. If you do, you are just setting yourself up for failure. What happens is you start to practice divorce. You will get really good at giving up on relationships if you start young, because the guy you are dating is probably not who you'll marry. The only other option is breaking up. Save yourself the heartache, refocus your desires on God and save the dating for later.

Hayley

PurpleSoul,

Dating. No, nothing for it or against it. But, know when you get into it, girls are looking for acceptance and guys are looking for sex. And girls will give in on sex to feel the acceptance of the guy. I know, "There are exceptions." Whatever! Just know that when you start trying to win the approval of a guy, he is looking for something in return.

Justin

Read Jeremiah 29:11 for God's promises about your future.

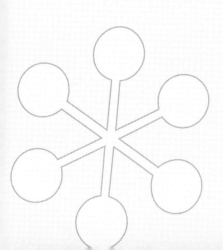

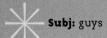

Posted by: Britney

If you really like a guy and you know that he doesn't like you and everything, is it wrong to pray about it?

Dear Britney,

It's never wrong to pray for God's will to be done. And it's not wrong to talk to God about things that are important to you. What is wrong is when you start to spend so much time praying to God about him that what you are really doing is fantasizing about the guy. You have to guard your heart and the best way to do that is to ask God to give you His best. That's what He wants to do, and He will do it if you will wait on Him. Don't put all your energy into converting a guy who doesn't like you into one that does. God is much better at this stuff than you. If He wants this guy to like you, He will make it happen. So pray, but don't pray about it all the time, go to God once with it, trust Him to take it from there, then get on with your life. If you don't, you are just giving your heart false hope and giving the enemy a chance to sneak in and make you bitter and angry if you don't get what you want.

Hayley

Britney,

Why would you? I am all about praying and even praying for things you really want. But, if you start praying that God will give you this dude, it will consume you. You will be thinking about it. Dreaming about it. Praying about it. You will do everything you can to try to get the dude to like you. And you won't like the answer when God says no. So you are putting yourself in a situation of ignoring God rather than listening to him. Pray about other things. Pray that you will become the person God wants you to be. When that happens, you will attract the person God want you to have.

Justin

Check this out: Phil. 4:6–9.

Posted by: Scared

Ok. This guy that I don't like keeps asking me 4 sex. What should I do? The only way to stop him from asking is to have sex with him. I need help. What should I do? I really need help on what to do. Please help me ASAP.

Dear Scared,

If this guy has some kind of control over you that would **force** you to have sex with him then that is **rape** and you need to tell someone right away. Tell a teacher, counselor, parent, pastor, police. This isn't something that you should try to fight yourself.

But if all he is doing is asking, then he has no control over you. **You** are the only one who has control over whether or not you say yes (unless he attacks you). But the idea that he is just pressuring you verbally is no reason to give in. Remember, only **you** control your actions. No one can control your decisions, or emotions, or your sex life. If he keeps bothering you, you have to tell someone. It's called "stalking" in legal terms and he could end up being a danger to you. Only **you** know if he is dangerous or not. If you think he's just a jerk bugging you, then tell him to leave you alone. But if you think he is dangerous, tell someone right away.

Hayley

Scared,

OK, this guy you don't like is asking you for sex. Get away
from him! You must be putting yourself close to where he
is, otherwise he wouldn't have the chance to hound you.
So do whatever it takes to get away. If he is a friend or a
friend of a friend, ditch the friends if you have to. Let them
know why. Don't leave it in the dark. Expose him. And
then, stay away from him.

Justin

Read 1 Peter 1:15–16.

Posted by: jerk

I did something that I shouldn't have and now I think I have lost a friend. I have asked forgiveness but she won't even talk to me. Since she's a Christian, shouldn't she forgive me and everything is cool? I feel lousy.

Dear jerk,

Now your **friend's** being the jerk. You did your job. You asked for forgiveness. You can't FORCE her to forgive you. Sorry. Wish I had a better answer than that.

Justin

Dear jerk,

That's tough, but I agree with Justin, you can't control her. You can repent and tell her you're sorry. But you can't make her get over it. Forgiveness doesn't release you, it releases them. So they will be in a prison until they let it go. But for you, keep earning the trust. Take the role of a servant. Do whatever you can to give your friend love, support, respect. Do this anyway, whether they get over it or not.

Hayley

Check out Luke 6:27–36 and 2 Corinthians 5:9–10 for more on this topic.

Posted by: 4-Christ
Will we know each other in heaven? Like would we think of
*NSYNC and all of the famous people as famous people? Would
I know my sisters and family?

Dear 4-Christ,

We don't really know all the particulars of heaven, but we could
make a guess based on the resurrected body of Jesus. He must have
been a bit different after he died and rose again, 'cause the disciples
didn't know who he was at first. Of course, who would have expected
to see Jesus after he had just been buried 3 days earlier? But after
they really looked at him they knew who he was. So we can surmise
from that that our heavenly bodies will be similar to our present
bodies, only better. We will be able to hug, and touch and stuff like
that. People will recognize us but we will be in glorified bodies.
Healthy, whole, happy. That's the best guess I have.

Hayley

4-Christ,

I am trying to forget *NSYNC now. I don't think that Jesus being
recognized by his disciples proves anything. If he would have
shown up in his heavenly form, they wouldn't have known who or
even what he was. So, no, I don't think we are going to be running
around looking like we do now. I think we are going to know others
by their essence. We will know them by who they are deeply. I
think we will be able to touch and communicate, but not with arms
and mouths. Don't ask me how it will happen, I don't have a clue.

Justin

Posted by: Michele

I found out that my friend, who is 15, sells and smokes weed. I'm very upset and confused. Doesn't he know he's hurting himself? I have no idea what to do, or what to say. What should I do? What should I say? Should I try to help him?

Dear Michele,

This is tough. Chances are he does know it's wrong. I mean it's illegal, hard to miss that part. If he is a believer you can talk to him about obeying the law, as we are told to do, but there is obviously a bigger issue here. I call it medication. Whatever it is—drugs, booze, movies, shopping—whatever we go to to cover up some kind of pain we have is called medication. And medication just dulls the effect of pain so we don't have to confront it. Trouble is God wants us to confront our pain, to live through it, not medicate our way through it.

Your best bet is to find out more about him. What's up in his life? Does he have problems? Does he know that God has a purpose for his life and pot will destroy that? Love him like Jesus would. Be there for him, but you can't hang out with him and get involved in this stuff. Talk to a pastor and have him talk with your friend. It's better for a guy to talk to him than a girl. Guys are funny that way. But don't use

this as an opportunity to gossip about someone. Be faithful to God and to your friend. And as I always say, your strongest weapon is prayer. Pray your heart out.

Hayley

Dear Michele,

Here's an idea. Throw an anonymous tip to the police. Leave it with the campus police. Then he will get busted and you can be there to help him through the hard times. It's not a bad thing. You are helping him in the long run. Just do not tell anyone what you did. It could get back to him and blow any chance you have to help.

Justin

Read Romans 12:9-12.

Posted by: J-Girl

If I have sex with my boyfriend and I'm not saved, will God 4-give me when I get saved? I'm waiting to get saved so that I can have sex with my boyfriend. So what? I mean, so what will happen? Please help me.

Dear J-Girl,

There are three issues here: 1. Your salvation 2. Forgiveness 3. Sex.

Let's start with 1: Don't try to be perfect *before* you get saved, the perfecting comes *after* you get saved. Ask Christ into your heart and then deal with the other stuff. Keep the main thing, the main thing, and that is Christ dying on a cross for you so that you can have access to the Father and a place in heaven, if you will only accept it. If you wait 'til you are perfect before you accept Him you will never accept Him. In fact, none of us would.

2. Forgiveness: God only forgives those who believe in Him and make Him Lord of their life. Once we confess with our mouths and believe in our hearts that Jesus is Lord we are forgiven for all we have done and all we will do, but that doesn't get us out of the discipline part. We still have to deal with what he allows to happen to us as a result of our disobedience, like pregnancy, disease, broken hearts—stuff like that.

OK, now for 3: Sex. You obviously know that sex outside marriage is wrong or you wouldn't be asking about forgiveness. So let me ask you this, why are you having sex with this guy? To make him like you? To fill an empty space in your heart? Do you know that sex completely changes your life? Statistically there is a 99% chance that this is **not** the guy you are going to marry. So now you've taken away from your future husband what should have been his. And if you *do* get knocked up know that nearly 80% of fathers of babies born to teen mothers **do not** marry their babies' mothers. Some 90% of these girls drop out of school and go on welfare. Their lives are forever marred by this one little thrill.

Don't become a statistic. Figure out why you are doing something you know is wrong. Do you do other things you know are wrong? Do you expect success in your life by doing the wrong thing? You can make a decision today to change your habits. They are all in your control. Are you going to let your desires control you, or your mind? It's your choice.

Hayley

Hey J-Girl,
I am going to spit in your face next week. Not just once but every day next week. In fact, I am going to rub it all over your face. But, I don't mean it. I am going to tell you I'm sorry. And I expect you to forgive me, OK? But, I don't really care about that right now. I really want to spit in your face. Is that OK? That is what you just asked. Think about it. Only you asked it about God. You know he is powerful. You know he sent his Son to die so you could be forgiven. You know that he is full of forgivness as well as fury. So why don't you ask God, the Creator, "God, I want to go have sex. I want to spit in your face. God, I don't care what you say right now. But, I am going to ask for forgiveness, OK?" See what he says.

Justin

Look at what Jesus says about following Him: John 12:25-26.

Posted by: Renee

Okay, my friend has always been against liking this guy. Well all of a sudden she is dating him. We used to be best friends but now we don't even talk or speak; it has only been less than a month. Me and another friend (also hangs with the first gurl), we know he is the wrong guy for her and she knows it too but she is not admitting it. She used to date this one guy, they were perfect—both Christians and everything, loved the same sports, the whole nine yards. She broke up with him and we don't know what happened. The guy she is currently dating is not for her. He is not who he proposes to be. I know he is trying to change b/c of her but he is making her come away from two of her best friends.

Dear Renee,

There are two things in life: things you can control and things you can't. The things you can control have to do with your will, your life. Like you can control how much you eat, or work out, or if you study, or shop. Stuff like that. But the things you can't control, like what other people do or think drain your energy away from what you can control. A life of faith is a life that knows what it can and can't control. The stuff that it can't control, it gives over to the Father. I know it sucks that she has strayed. And I wish there was a magic way for you to change her back, but each person is in control of their own will (thank God) and she has chosen a different path.

My suggestion to you is to take it to the one who *can* change her. Pray. Pray like crazy. Ask the Father to show her what *she* needs to see. Love her, even though she walks away from you.

One final note, don't turn prayer for her into an excuse to talk about her. That's gossip cloaked as a prayer request. Keep it between God and you. He knows the deal. You are faithful. He will honor you. Keep up the faith! I'm proud of you.

Hayley

Renee,

You really don't have to do anything. The relationship will not last. Hey, when you are 14, 15, 16 even 18 years old, know that the relationship will not last. Look, it's only been a month. Give it another month or so and she will be split from him. Hopefully, she won't get too messed up (pregnant, disease, depression) during the process. Just be her friend and be there for her when it ends.

Justin

Take a look at Jeremiah 17:7–8.

Posted by: J.R.
My boyfriend wants me to have sex with him. I know I should say no, but if I do he will dump me. I really like him, and I don't want to break up with him. What should I tell him? Something else you should know is that he is a Christian too. Why is sex the only thing that guys think about? I need answers. Please help me; I need to know what to do.

Dear J.R.,

You should tell him that you two just aren't meant for each other because you thought you were dating a godly guy, and a godly guy wouldn't obey his feelings over his God. Some men think about sex all the time. But, if you are wanting a relationship that honors God, you need to find a guy that doesn't. If a man is pressuring you to do anything immoral is God pleased?

Do you want to live outside God's will just to keep a guy who isn't faithful?

Remember, if he will do it for you, he will do it to you. So if he will have sex outside marriage with you, he will very, very likely have sex outside marriage with someone else. He is showing you his character by demanding you sin against your Lord.

And remember this, boys want you 'til they get you. If you still want to keep dating him, remember that he will like you much, much more if you *don't* sleep with him. Read 2 Samuel 13, and see how men's emotions change. It is unhealthy in a relationship for one person to always be the "gatekeeper," to always be the one making sure you're honoring God in your relationship. Hold out for someone who respects you and loves God enough to honor him with your relationship.

Consider the character of the guys you date. Make a list. If your list includes the following: liar, immoral, lustful, pressuring, and unfaithful, then look no further—you've found your guy. If your list includes faithful, honest, and godly, then start lookin' for him. Stay strong. God is watching and waiting to see which you will choose.

Hayley

J.R.,
First know this. Your relationship will end. Sleeping with a guy will only put off the breakup. So you will give in, compromise and then you will have to live with the pain. So it's really up to you. See, guys will lie to get what they want. And what they want is sex (even the Christian ones). They will tell you they love you. That you make them feel like they can do anything. They will tell you that you were meant to be together. They will even talk about your future together, when you are married. They are trying to reassure you that the two of you will be married so you will be OK with giving up the sex now (because you are getting married anyway). But he really doesn't think you will be together forever. Even if you ask him about it he will assure you that you will be together. Whatever.

So, get out. He doesn't care about you that much. Guess what? He will do the exact same thing to his next girlfriend. He is going to have sex with her and it won't be special with her just like it won't be special with you.

Justin

Read Jude 1:24–25.

Posted by: Maggie

My Mom thinks that romantic movies and romance novels aren't good for me. All my other friends get to go to them how come I can't?

Dear Maggie,

You're Mom's kinda right on this one. Not that I hate romance or anything, but when you are not married it's kind of dangerous. I call it female porn. It's porn to us cuz it's just like porn is to men. Guys are turned on by naked girls. And girls are turned on by romantic guys. So if naked girls is porn for guys, then romance movies is porn for girls.

It gets us all excited about the perfect man, the perfect love and it makes us judge all guys based on the super amazing ones in the movies and in books. It's just like guys judging you based on the babes they see in porn mags. It also makes you totally long for what you can't have yet. It makes you feel depressed cuz you don't have a relationship like that. Don't deny it. When you walk out of a chick flick you think, "Dang, why can't I get a guy like that?"

So maybe your Mom has something on this one. And besides, she's your Mom, til you're 18 you have to listen to her.

Hayley

Maggie,

Oh yeah. Way bad. Guys are not perfect. We mess up. We say the wrong things. We do stupid things. The guys in movies and novels, even when they screw up, they seem so charming. What you feed your mind is what you become. And no, this doesn't mean you become a romantic. It means you become a failure in love, because you have these standards in your mind that no guy can live up to. Instead of God making man in his image, you are trying to make man into the image you want him to be.

Justin

Posted by: Clarissa
There's this black guy at school who wants to go out with me, but I'm white and I'm afraid I'm not supposed to go out with him. Does God allow people from other races to date?

Dear Clarissa,

In the Old Testament God warned the people not to intermarry with different cultures. This didn't mean different races but different religions. The people of other religions worshiped idols, not God. And God can't stand for that kind of mixture of evil with good. In the New Testament He tells us not to be unequally yoked, which means don't marry someone who doesn't have the same faith as you (II Corin. 6:14). God honored the interracial marriage of Ruth and Boaz. He doesn't care about the color of skin, but the condition of your heart.

Hayley

Clarissa,
Yes.

Justin

Posted by: sun goddess
What is appropriate for girls to wear? I've been told I can't wear tube tops and mini skirts? But is it ok to wear a tankini top bathing suite that hardly shows your belly button? What is going too far?

Dear sun goddess,
It depends on what your goal is. If you want to use your body as a tool to get what you want then show it all off. But if you would rather not manipulate or control men by the use of your body then you might want to consider another option.

Hayley

sun goddess,
What is going too far? is not the question. What is appropriate is the real deal. You are going to be treated the way you look. If you look like a sexy little thing with all your business showing, then you will get treated like a piece of meat. Face it, guys stare at girls. When you wear something revealing, every guy from 8 to 80 is looking at you. So when you get dressed and look in the mirror remember, your grandfather and all his old friends are looking at your body. Is that what you want them to see?

Justin

Posted by: Serenity

I'm totally unclear on the subject of dating. I've always been more of a tomboy type of gal, definitely not into the whole mushy crush stuff. Well that was about 3 months ago. There's this guy that I totally dig. The thing is I don't want to date, he's 18 (I'm 14), and well he likes me. He is unsaved, which sends off flares that say keep your guard up girl. And I do. My mind wanders a lot to him.

Dear Serenity,

Good girl. Glad you see flares. If an 18-year-old guy is interested in at 14-year-old girl look out. He's up to no good. Sorry to say it but that's the truth. He is a man looking at girls. Not cool. Definitely sexual. Especially if he's a non-believer. Check out I Corinthians 6:14 for more on that!

You have to control your thoughts about him. I know it's hard but you can do it. Don't fantasize or daydream about him, it only fuels the fire. I believe that dating is OK for people who are ready to get married. And you definitely aren't!

If you date when you aren't ready for marriage you are just setting yourself up for trouble and pain. Breaking up sucks! You don't want to go through that, and every time you do you are just practicing divorce.

The Bible never talks about dating, because it never

happened. People only sought a mate to fulfill their purpose, not for lust, or giggles, or love or any of that. Don't let your emotions choose your destiny. You are doing right. You are asking the right questions. Just stay strong and avoid older men!

Hayley

Serenity,

Flip the roles. You are 18. Would you go out with someone who is 14? C'mon. Really. Don't play the "it depends" role. The answer is NO. So, why does an 18 year old guy want to go out with a 14 year-old girl? Well, first, he is uncomfortable with girls his own age. He wants to be in a relationship where he can control it. He knows that he can manipulate you easier and get you to like him. He knows that you will automatically like him more because he is an "older guy". And the extreme reason, especially since he is not a Christian, is sex. He knows that being so much older, it makes you easier prey. He can convince younger girls that he is right a lot easier than he can with older girls. This has nothing to do with any flaws in you. You stay where you are and be the best 14 year-old you can be. Stay away from him because he has personal issues.

Justin

Posted by: Nicole

I am really good friends with a guy in my class. We were partners on a project in school and some of my friends kind of got the wrong idea . . . if ya know what I mean?! We tried telling them that we are just friends, but no one seems to listen...I'd really appreciate some advice on what to tell my friends. Ok . . . just to add to all this, I do have a crush on him (I don't want anyone to know). I think he knows, but I just keep trying to tell my friends otherwise. A lot of my friends say he likes me too. Should I just stay friends or should I find out if he really likes me. . . . I don't know what to do. I need a lot of advice on a confusing thing . . .

Dear Nicole,

Here's my prescription for you. Tell your friends that sure you think he's cute but you are just friends. They don't need to be getting into your business like that. Let them joke or whatever but just let it go with we're just friends, because you are. Don't make a big deal about it. Now as for the guy, NO do not pursue him. God designed guys to be the aggressor. When girls start to take that role from guys, they make them feel like wimps. If this guy likes you then he will let you know, but just give him time. You can give him clues. You can flirt and be nice to him, but don't take matters into your own hands. This is your test before God. Will you trust God to run things the way He designed them?

Guy pursuing girl. Or will you tell God He's too slow, and take control yourself? God is waiting to see what you will do.

Nicole,

As for your friends, it's none of their biz. They can say whatever they want, just ignore it.

For the guy. Are you tired of being his friend? Because if you connect with him and you start trying the whole dating thing, your friendship is over. It will never be the same. So if you are totally tired of being friends, go for it. If you really enjoy the friendship, don't make a move. Enjoy it.

Subj: Dull faith

Posted by: SuperLeslie

My spiritual life just seems so dull and boring. Almost like there's a cloud and God's behind it, ya know? I mean, I pray, I read my Bible, I go on just like it was before, and there's nothing. Nothing. Nada. Zip. I feel almost like He's gone, but I know He's not. It's been like this for sooo long.

Dear Leslie,

You are in a place called the desert. We all go through it. It's dry, dull and lifeless. Seems like God isn't there. But don't let feelings be your guide.

You have a job to do in the desert. It's the place where your faith is tested. Do you only love Him because you feel Him, or because you know Him? I want you to read *Hinds Feet on High Places* by Hannah Hurnard. It's about the place you are in.

Take heart, this will pass, but you must remain faithful and love Him even though you don't feel it.

Hayley

Leslie,

I have an idea for you. Don't read your Bible. That's right. Don't do it for a month. We get into this whole, I have to read the Bible 20 minutes a day because that is what a good Christian does. Whatever. If you are not getting anything

Ask **Both of Us**

out of it and are just going through the motions, don't do it. I just went on a four week Bible fast (sounds weird but hang with me). I was bored and just reading the Bible and not really getting into it. I pick up the Word two days ago, and I haven't been able to put it down. It is fresh. Alive. I was so hungry for it that I am devouring the Word of God.

Justin

Posted by: Maz

I'm a Christian and i luv God and have a good relationship with Him. Why should i bother to get baptised???

Dear Maz,

Cuz the Bible says to!

Justin

Dear Maz,

As Justin so eloquently put it, the Bible says so! Baptism is just a symbol of your commitment to Christ. Like a wedding ring on your mom and dad. If you are too afraid to get in front of people and confess your faith like that then you probably aren't saved. It's just a way to show people what you believe. And hey, Jesus did it, so I'm doin it too!

Hayley

Subj: older guy

Dear Little Girl,

It depends how young and how old. As you get older, age becomes less of a problem, because you are both adults and have lots of life experiences. But if you are still pretty young and he is an adult, then there is something wrong.

See a man should not want to hang out with a girl. If he wants to then he probably has some issues. He might seem just perfect but looks can be deceiving. Here's how to tell. Tell him you just want to be friends and see how he reacts. If he acts like a jerk then you'll know that he's not the one. If he acts cool then you can give it some time. Wait til you are both adults and age isn't such a biggie.

Hayley

Little Girl,

If you like older guys, that means you are like all girls. At some time they are all crushing on older hotties. But, from the guy's perspective, being older and then going out with a younger girl is easier on every level. They let us get away with more stuff. We don't have to be as strong or as much of a leader. And yes, they are easier sexually. Younger girls are easier to con and get them to compromise. So if you are looking at older guys, know that these are the reasons they are looking at you.

Justin

Posted by: smile2001

Do you know where in the Bible I can find the book that talks about mildew, because a non-Christian in my class doesn't think you can take the Bible seriously when there is a book in it talking about mildew. But I want to prove her wrong by showing her the great bits of the Bible to encourage her. I would just like to read the part she is talking about for myself.

Dear Smile2001,

Leviticus 14: 33–48

Deuteronomy 28:22

Amos 4:9

Haggai 2:17

Hope that helps!

Hayley

Smile2001,

Wow, I have never heard of mildew being a way to talk to your friends about Christ. But hey, whatever works. Keep going. Not to prove your friends wrong, but to try to hook them into the Scripture.

There are other passages in the Bible that deal with crazy things, such as the donkey that talks, Saul pooping in the sheep pen, and the sex scandal of King David. Read Numbers 22:22–40, 1 Samuel 24:3, and 2 Samuel 11 to find out more about these stories.

Justin

Dear Fishgirl,

We don't know for sure what Bathsheba was thinking when David called her into the castle that night. We do know that you didn't refuse a king. So she would have had to sleep with him no matter what she wanted to do. But also he was a hottie AND she was bathing outside where she knew the King could see her, soooo. . . . We also know that she mourned the death of her husband. So she probably loved him and didn't want to hurt him. Keep in mind that in those days women were stoned for adultery, so chances are this wasn't her choice.

Hayley

Dear Fishgirl,

My question is what was she doing taking a bath where she knew she could be seen? I don't know about the force issue, but she was playing with fire. It's like girls that wear tight shirts and short shorts and then act surprised when all guys want from them is sex. Well, that's what you are showing. Sex. Don't act shocked. I don't think Bathsheba was shocked.

Justin

Read the story in 2 Samuel 11.

Posted by: Clarity
What do you think about human cloning. I'm totally against it, how 'bout you?

Dear Clarity,

Human cloning is man's attempt to prove that we don't need God. We are strong enough and smart enough to make life on our own. Trouble is they can't make life without existing life. They don't create another animal from nothing, they use existing DNA. So they aren't really creating life.

Scientists are using cloning to create better and safer products for us. They are using what they learn right now, for good, but it could be perverted when we try to make human clones. The moral dilemma comes when we try to create a human race to our liking. We determine what traits are best and make people in our image. It is a very dangerous toy to play with. But know that they can't do anything without God allowing it. So we have nothing to fear. God sees what they are doing and will allow all to unfold according to His will.

Dear Clarity,

All for it. Just think. They could grow like crops of kidneys or whatever they needed to help people. Now, I am not for the human cloning thing. One of me is enough. But it has some great uses.

Justin

Read more about similar topics: Genesis 11:1–9, Psalm 139:13–16, and Job 42:2.

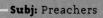

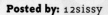

Posted by: 12sissy

Why do you think that preachers tend to wear black all the time? I know it might just be a fad or a fave color (which I could not stand, lol!), but what's your opinion?

Dear Sissy,

Priests actually began to dress differently in order *not* to be in fashion. In 428 A.D. Pope Celestine rebuked bishops for wearing clothes that made them stand out, and laid down the rule that "we [the bishops and clergy] should be distinguished from the common people by our learning, not by our clothes; by our conduct, not by our dress; by cleanness of mind, not by the care we spend upon our person[3]." They wore the long plain clothes that were worn by the humbler class so as not to be proud. Black isn't gaudy or trendy, it's simple and doesn't call a lot of attention to the person wearing it. In psychology, the color black also implies submission to God.

Hayley

Sissy,

I think it's because they have NO fashion sense. My pastor would show up with different color socks and a tie that wasn't even from the same generation as the shirt he was wearing. So I loved it when he would go with basic black. Plus, it slimmed his hips down a little.

Justin

Posted by: Brittany

Okay, I have been thinking about this for so long and I have yet to come to a conclusion and it seems like no one can help because everyone feels differently about it and they all confuse me. So the Q is: Who created capital punishment?? God? Or the people / government???

I'm so confused because in the Bible it says: Thou shalt not kill. Then it goes on and says in Exodus chapter 21 verses 12-27: If A man strikes a man causing him to die then the attacker is allowed to be put to death . . . So!?!?! HELP!

I mean doesn't that sorta contradict itself? I am by no means doubting the Bible. It's just I'm really confused?!?!

Dear Brittany,

The deal is this, we have to look at the Old Testament through the eyes of the New one. Before Christ came to save us the Israelites were expected to be perfect. If they did something wrong then there had to be a sacrifice. And the sacrifice for murder was death. The law was very clear on that. Once Christ came he was the final and ultimate sacrifice for all sins so that we didn't have to do all those bloody sacrifices any more. There are now 2 kinds of law, moral and civil. The 10 Commandments are our moral law. This law still stands as truth. Christ did not erase any of the law; he only fulfilled it by being the sacrifice for all our sins. But all through the Old Testament you will find the civil law like in Leviticus. These were really strict codes the Israelites had to follow to please God. Jesus asks us to now follow the law of the country in which we live and not to strictly follow the civil law in the Old Testament.

That still leaves us with a decision to make as believers. The sixth commandment says "Thou shall not commit murder." Some say that means we can't kill criminals. But murder is different from killing. Murder is unlawfully killing with malice and pre-meditation. That's why some say that capital punishment is OK. It is not unlawful and it isn't with malice.

Others say that it isn't our right to decide what kind of punishment people get for sin.

There is no black and white here. Both sides have valid arguments. And as believers we have to make a decision for ourselves.

Hayley

Brittany,

Capital punishment. God created it. In Genesis, Adam and Eve sinned and they were kicked out of the Garden and sentenced to death. It wasn't immediate. They still lived a while. Kind of like they were on death row. So yeah, God is all about grace and he is all about punishment. He has put us as humans in charge of carrying out both.

Justin

"There is a time to kill and a time to heal" (Ecclesiastes 3:3a).

Posted by: Beth

Did God make the world in six literal days, and if so, how? As the sun wasn't created, who could define a day? And what about tectonics and stuff? Weren't they supposed to have taken millions of years?

Dear Beth,

Christians debate many things and this is one of them. We can debate all day long and it won't change the main thing, and that is that God so loved the world that He gave His only begotten son as a sacrifice that we might be saved. Whatever the discussion on old earth/young earth know that God is always God, no matter what is decided and that Jesus died for you.

But to answer your question, we don't have a solid answer. It is a matter of faith and science, which don't have to disagree. Some choose to believe that every word in the English Bible is literal. Therefore a 'day' equals 24 hours. And why can't God create the earth in just 7 days, He's God?

Others say that in the original language 'one day' meant one generation. Therefore it took much longer than 7 earth days to create the earth.

Either way we can see from the text that the order in which He created earth is completely scientific.

Everything was created in the proper order. Whatever you choose to believe, don't let this discussion overshadow Christ's death on a cross. Whether the earth is old or new doesn't change the fact that Christ is our only hope and salvation.

For more info on this go to a website called www.reasonstobelieve.com. Hugh Ross has lots of info on science and faith. You can also go to http://www.talkorigins.org/faqs/gish-ross-debate.html to read a debate between Hugh Ross and Duane Gish, a young-earth proponent.

Read Genesis 1 and 2 to learn more about Creation.

Hayley

Dear Beth,

I think God had a huge microwave that he put the world in. Kind of like a big baked potato. In the oven it would take a couple of hours. In the microwave, 15 minutes. Same with the world. Yeah, but normal human time means it would take a million years. In God's super-sized microwave, ZAP, 6 days.

Justin

Posted by: Liz

What is the point of life? Isn't being a Christian just meant to benefit u after u die???

Dear Liz,

That's a bonus. And that's usually the reason people get saved. We are completely selfish before we get saved and accept Christ to make our lives better or just to get to heaven. But once we fall in love with God we start to realize that it's not just about us and our eternity. That's why Paul said he would gladly give up his own salvation if it would mean others could be saved.

The real point of life is for us to fall in love with God and then a funny things happen: more purposes for our life start to show up. When you love someone you want to start doing whatever you can to make them happy. And it makes God really happy when you love His creation. So your purpose becomes to love God and to love others. Suddenly that means all kinds of things. You want to lead them to Christ, you want to feed them, to forgive them, to help them. You start to care a lot about others. Suddenly your purpose in life is huge. It becomes much less about you and much more about love.

God created us cuz He had so much love and wanted to share it not just to save us. So the point of life is to love Him and to love others as you love yourself.

Liz,

If you let Christianity just benefit you when you die, what a waste of good Christianity. Once you have given your life to Jesus as your Lord, that is where real life begins. John 10:10 says, "I have come to give you life and life to the fullest." That means anything you could see and experience without God, He wants to amp it up and let you really experience it. It is the difference in riding a tricycle (before Christ) and flying a fighter-jet at the top speed. They are both transportation, but WOW! what a difference. Dive into Christianity and your life will go full throttle.

Justin

"Love the Lord your God will all your heart, all your soul, and all your strength" (Deuteronomy 6:4).

Posted by: Mary-Girl

I don't understand. All I want is music with a good message. Something that speaks to you and really, I don't find that in Christian music. It mostly sounds pre-packaged to me. It's not that I am against it, or am a Satanist or anything, but I don't really enjoy it. I am sick of people telling me I am wrong about everything, it only makes me feel like I am more alone. I have tried to find Christian rock music that I like, and so far it really falls short.

Dear Mary-Girl,

I totally don't blame you, Christian music can really miss the point. It doesn't always have all the emotion we need, and feel, just like some secular music doesn't really vibe with us. I don't think there is anything wrong with listening to non-Christian music if the message is good. A lot of love songs that were written about men and women, really sound like they are written about God. So who's to say?

Have you tried PAX 217, AudioAdrenaline or Skillet? There is some good Christian metal like POD and some rock stuff like Creed. Check these bands out—you might hear some stuff you like.

Mary-Girl,

AMEN! I have tried too. Yeah, when I am in the mood I can get into the christian music thing. But for the most part it's

just not my vibe. There are friends, family, even well
meaning youth ministers that will tell you you're wrong for
listening to other stuff. But I love what Wes King, a
christian music artist, said one time. He said there is no
such thing as christian music.

Justin

"Brothers and sisters, think about the things that are good
and worthy of praise. Think about the things that are true and
honorable and right and pure and beautiful and respected"
(Philippians 4:8).

Note

If you have a question you want to ask Hayley or Justin,
visit www.xt4j.com and check out their bulletin board.

Dateable: Are they? Are you?
by Justin Lookadoo
0-7852-6433-7
$12.99

Hands and Feet
by AudioAdrenaline
0-7180-0171-0
$15.99

Step Off: the hardest 30 days
of your life
Adventure Guide
by Justin Lookadoo
0-7852-4604-5
$9.99

Extreme Teen Bible
0-7180-0164-8
$19.99

AUDIO ADRENALINE

Put four crazy friends together, throw in some music and blend on the highest speed and you get Audio Adrenaline. These guys are best known for radio hits like "Big House" and "Mighty Good Leader" and they keep on cranking 'em out on their latest CD, *LIFT*. We'd like to offer you a deal to pick up a copy of the CD using the attached coupon. If you already have it in your collection, feel free to give the coupon to a friend who is missing out on the action.

For the latest

AUDIO ADRENALINE

info, check out

www.audioa.com

to see pictures,

hear music,

buy merch

and get

tour updates.

Check it out! Get involved! Make a difference!

Habitat for Humanity International
A Christian organization and welcomes volunteers
from all faiths who are committed to Habitat's goal
of eliminating poverty housing.
www.habitat.org

National Center for Family Literacy
Promoting family literacy services
across the United States.
www.famlit.org

Chernobyl Children's Project
Help improve the quality of life of the kids affected
by the Chernobyl radiation.
www.adiccp.org

Volunteer Match
Enter your zip code in this search engine, and
it will tell you all the volunteer opportunities
in your neighborhood.
www.volunteermatch.org

Ask **Hayley,** *Ask* **Justin**

Ask **Hayley,** *Ask* **Justin**

Nelson Reference and Electronic Publishing
Nashville
a division of Thomas Nelson, Inc.
www.thomasnelson.com
www.xt4J.com

Ask Hayley, Ask Justin
Written by Hayley Morgan and Justin Lookadoo
Copyright © 2002 by Thomas Nelson, Inc.

Extreme for Jesus™ Acquisitions Editor: Kate Etue
Cover Design by Kate Etue
Interior Page Design by Lori Lynch/Book & Graphic Design, Thomas Nelson, Inc.
Editorial guidance provided by: Beth Ann Patton and Jamie Menzie

Published in Nashville, Tennessee, by Thomas Nelson, Inc.

ISBN 0-7180-0162-1

Library of Congress Cataloging-in-Publication Data

Printed in the United States of America
1 2 3 4 5 — 06 05 04 03 02

Hayley Morgan is the successful developer of Extreme for Jesus™, a line of more than thirty books and Bibles that have sold over 1,000,000 units. An ex-Nike manager, her flare for understanding teens is unsurpassed. Her first book, *Extreme Encounters*, is the best-selling book in the Xt4J brand.

Ask **Hayley**

Posted by: Kelsey

Well, I'm confused because the Bible says I'm supposed to be loving my enemies. Does this mean I'm supposed to love Satan? It's really been bothering me. Please help.

Dear Kelsey,

The answer is no, we are not to love Satan. Satan is the enemy of God. He is more than a foe to us; he is evil itself and as children of light we cannot love darkness or have any part in it. Since there is nothing good at all in Satan, there is nothing in him that we can love. Humans, on the other hand, are made in the likeness of God and therefore we are to love them, even if it seems impossible.

Generally we have enemies because of sinfulness, covetousness, anger, envy, greed, pride—things like that. As believers our best defense against sin is love. Love doesn't practice sinfulness, so if we wish to combat sin, we have to love others. To hate them, to envy them, or to wish them harm is directly opposed to love.

Read Matthew 22:37–40 for more.

Posted by: curious

I found my grandmother's Catholic Bible the other day. I know that there are added books, but I thought it would be interesting to read them. I know they aren't God's inspired Word, so can I read them?

Dear Curious,

Catholics believe that these "added" books are the inspired Word of God. Protestants believe that they are only writings from the same time period, but not the Word of God.

If you are a Protestant and you read these books, you need to look at them as any other book you might read, but not as Scripture. You will find many things in them that don't agree with what you believe, so be ready to get answers. Go into it with the thought that it will be interesting, but not inspired.

If your parents are Protestants, you might want to talk it over with them before you do anything.

"I did not speak in secret or hide my words in some dark place . . . I am the Lord, and I speak the truth; I say what is right" (Is. 45:19).

Posted by: Rachel

I'm nearly 14 and I have never even had a boyfriend. Am I the only one??? I want a Christian boyfriend but I don't actually know any Christian boys!!! All the people in my class must think I'm pathetic!!!

Dear Rachel,

Don't listen to 'em; you are totally normal. The world has gotten all messed up about what is important. God never once mentions the importance of dating, does He? In fact, He never once mentions dating. Don't let what the world thinks is important be important to you. You live by a different set of rules than most people. You live by God's law. God wants you to seek Him first and He'll give you all the rest in good time.

You are not trying to win the approval of men, but the approval of God (Galatians 1:10). Don't give into the pressure of the world because you want its approval. In the end you'll save yourself a ton of heartache. While all your friends are breaking up and crying over it, you will be happy and whole. You have plenty of time to date, enjoy what God has given you right now and take your focus off of the peer pressure.

Read these words of encouragement: Psalm 119:57-64.

Subj: troubled. what should i do?

Posted by: *angel*

Just about everyone in my entire school isn't a Christian, and all the time I hear swearing and dirty stuff and it's horrible, and whenever they hear the word *Christian* they think it's stupid!! I don't feel like telling anyone I'm a Christian or I'll get teased and mocked. What should I do? HELP!

Dear Angel,

Jesus said, "In this world you will have trouble" (John 16:33). He never said that life as a believer would be easy; in fact He said it would be hard. He also told us that we are the salt of the world. Have you ever felt salt in an open wound? It hurts awful! You are the salt, and you might make those kids mad, but you can't deny your faith or hide it. You are a lamp, Jesus says, and you aren't to hide a lamp under a blanket. It's supposed to light the darkness.

You are in the perfect place: the place of darkness. God put you there to be the light, not to hide the light. It is great that these kids are so nasty—it shows how much they need God. Nothing they say can hurt you, not their cussing or their slams. But what you don't do *can* hurt you. You are called to tell the world about Him even when they think He's stupid. Are you ready to do battle for the God you love? Or will you cower and hide Him from the very people who need Him?

Check out Matthew 5:13-16, John 15:18-23 and Ephesians 6:10-18 for some insight.

Posted by: Stephanie

Hey, my question is how do u tell a friend that's ur crush that ur in 2 him without ruining ur friendship?

Dear Stephanie,

You don't.

Sorry. You just don't tell him without it ruining your friendship. God made guys to be the leaders. That means that they lead in relationships. They tell you they like you. They call you. They ask you out. It is just an all around bad idea for girls to take away the guys' responsibility. It whacks out everything from then on. Be friends with him, let him figure out if he likes you or not just by being around you. Don't rush him and don't rush God. When it will work, if it will work, God will prompt the guy so he will know too. Wait on God.

Read Psalm 62:5-8 and Hebrews 13:20-21.

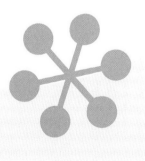

Posted by: *~Star~*

My friends swear and curse and one of them said that they don't care that they go to hell or not! Help me, this is a big problem!! What can I do to ignore them and act like a Christian without my friends noticing, or should I really tell them I'm a Christian and then never have any friends (because they would spread it around and then the whole school would make fun of me!!!!!)

Dear Star,

You have to make a choice between God and popularity. It's a hard choice, but you must make it now. Are you trying to please your friends or God? 'Cause God wants people to know you love Him. Are you so embarrassed of Him you have to hide Him? Don't you believe He loves you and knows what is best for you?

If the Bible is true, then you are actually totally blessed when they hate you, talk about you, and slam your name because you love God. You can't be a Christian and hide that fact. If you do, then you have chosen the world over God (1 John 2:15). So it's up to you. Is your rep more important than God and the lives of your friends?

Check out these verses to pump you up: Matthew 5:10–12; Matthew 28:16–20; John 4:35–36; Romans 10:14–17; 1 Corinthians 3:6–9.

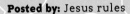

Subj: being a good Christian

Dear Jesus Rules,

What you have is a bad habit. That is something that you've allowed yourself to do so much that you now have a hard time stopping even though you know it's wrong. How do you change patterns in your life? Well, until *doing* the habit becomes more painful than *not* doing it, you won't ever stop.

So try writing down two paragraphs, one for each of these:

1. In 5 years if I keep telling lies, gossiping, and stuff like that my life will be like this . . .
2. In 5 years if I am no longer telling lies, gossiping, and stuff like that my life will be like this . . .

Be really honest. Be really creative. Then read these everyday. Your mind will become convinced that it hurts too much to sin like that anymore, and it will become easier to do what's right.

Take a look at these: Ephesians 4:29–32 and 2 Timothy 2:16.

Posted by: April

Hey, recently I went on vacation and begged to go to church before we had to leave the same day. Well, they had visitors stand up and say something. Low and behold, the pastor tells me that he senses a strong evangelical spirit within me. The only thing is . . . what exactly does this mean? I mean, a reserved person going out and sharing . . . it's all possible with God. Can I have some input???

Dear April,

Remember that the gifts of God aren't there because of our strength but because of His. If they were your strengths then you wouldn't need God. If the word from that pastor isn't news to you—that is, you have thought of it before—then he just might be right. A prophecy over you usually confirms stuff God is already showing you in His Word or in circumstances around you. God loves to talk to us through all sorts of avenues. Make sure you're looking to and listening for all of them.

So if you think you might have the gift of evangelism then nurture it. Learn about it. Talk to people, read books, and trust God to fulfill it in you. Remember, Moses couldn't talk very well and was totally sure God was off His rocker for calling him to save the Jews out of Egypt. Saul hid when they were trying to make him king. We don't always agree with God's assessment about us, but that doesn't mean He's wrong; it just means we need some faith and some practice.

Check these out: 1 Corinthians 12:1–11; Ephesians 4:11–13; 1 Peter 4:10.

Posted by: ~Lizzy~

Am I a bad person? I have been going out with this one guy for a while, but he is not a Christian. Is this bad? Should we break up because my values are different than his? Please Help Me!

Dear Lizzy,

Dating a non-believer is like playing with fire. God refuses to allow us to marry someone who doesn't believe in Him and dating often leads to marriage. So if you date a non-believer only two things can happen:

1. You break up, and that totally bites! The pain of breaking up is no fun for anyone.
2. You get married, and that totally bites because now you disobeyed God's law and will have to live with the consequences.

So looking at your only two options doesn't make dating a non-believer sound like a very wise decision. No matter what it's gonna totally bite!

It's best not to get involved in a love relationship with a non-believer 'cause a non-believer is someone who hates God. Time for you to choose. Will you choose God or this guy?

Check out 2 Corinthians 6:14–18.

Posted by: Suzie

Is fantasizing wrong? I sometimes imagine things about guys, not nasty things, but just wishing things would happen. I mean, I often think how good it would be if such and such happened so I could do something. Is that wrong?

Dear Suzie,

Jesus said that not only is adultery wrong but that looking at someone lustfully was just like sleeping with them. This means that God cares just as much about what you think as He does about what you do. If you know that your thoughts will be judged just as harshly as your actions, will that make you change what you think about?

It is no less a sin to think or fantasize about it than it is to actually do it. As soon as a bad thought comes into your mind you have to stop it. Temptation is not a sin, but turning that temptation into a fantasy that you think about over and over is a sin.

Check out Philippians 4:8-9 for encouragement.

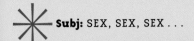

Posted by: Chiquita

I know you aren't supposed to have it before you're married, but is it OK to think about it? I talk about it with my friends; is that wrong? I really need to know because I don't want God to be mad at me for wondering about it a lot! It interests me and I like to think about it. Am I wrong?

Dear Chiquita,

There is no harm in wondering about sex. That's totally normal for teenagers. Sex is a beautiful gift that God has given to married people. To wonder is okay, to learn about it from a purely educational standpoint is okay too, but to fantasize about it, to think about doing it with someone, is the same as actually doing it with them.

So learn about sex, know that someday it will be great when you are married, but don't try to daydream about the person you want to have sex with. That is not yours to do. Check out Philippians 4:8-9 and 1 Thessalonians 4:1-8 for more insight.

Posted by: Godzgirl

What is your opinion about women wearing pants and makeup and cutting their hair and stuff that it says in the Bible women shouldn't do?

Dear Godzgirl,

What you have to know about Scripture is that some passages are what we call "prescriptive" (they tell us what to do today) and some are "descriptive" (they talk about Bible times). The authors of the Bible wrote to a people who lived two thousand years ago and had their own customs, laws, and ideas of social conduct. Because of this a lot of passages are descriptive—that is, they tell people in *that* society how to get along in *that* society. Paul says all things are permissible but not all things are beneficial. That means that if you do something and it causes a big problem for others, it's probably best you don't do it. So in these "descriptive" passages on women, Paul is talking to a church where women were getting out of hand. They were getting wild, and Paul had to talk to them so they would get some kind of order back again.

Today it is not a scandal for women to wear pants, makeup or to cut their hair. So no, those things are not considered sinful.

Read 1 Corinthians 10:23 and 1 Corinthians 11:6–15.

Ask **Hayley**　13

Posted by: Akalei

See, there is a guy on my street and God wants me to witness to him. Every time I try to talk about God, I can't get it out. What should I do?

Dear Akalei,

It's an amazing thing to hear from God. And it's even more amazing to actually do what He is asking you to do. But it's totally hard, I know. Don't get down on yourself. Just know this: every time that you respond to Him is another opportunity to grow your faith muscles. And the more those grow, the more faith He will give you.

If God wants you to witness to this guy, ask how He wants you to do that. Is it by being his friend and telling him about your relationship with Christ? Or is it by giving him a book? Or by just flat out asking him, "Do you know where you are going after you die?"

There are tons of conversation starters like that. People want to know where they will go when they die; it's human nature. And it's not offensive to ask that. Just be loving when it's your turn to talk. Share from your heart and trust God to be the One to draw him to Himself. God doesn't ask you to convert him, just to tell him.

You can do it or God wouldn't be asking you to. Take the leap of faith. Exercise your faith muscles and see what God will do.

For some good examples of faith, take a look at: Luke 17:6 and Hebrews 11.

Posted by: Christina
Sometimes I feel as if I'm living a double life. I don't hide being a Christian at school, but I do cuss a little (as hard as I try not to). At school I join in on the jokey-bashing (you know, where they know you're just playing), but at church I'm all "love everybody" and pretty much a model Christian—youth group prez and ultra-volunteer. I feel horrible when I realize I'm doing something that I wouldn't tell my Sunday school teacher. I know there are kids who live more of a double life than me, but that doesn't make mine right. Please help!!

Dear Christina,
You just helped yourself by admitting that there is a difference. This might sound corny, but the first step in change is to recognize that you need to change. Which you is the real you? The church girl or the school girl?

Here's the deal, now you have to figure out how to make the change to becoming one person. Start with prayer. Tell Him you know you've messed up and that you want to change. Expect Him to help you. But know that you have to work at it too. Now make a plan of action. Decide what you stand for, what your values are and who you want to be. Then find someone to hold you accountable.

Check these out: Romans 12:2 and 1 John 4:19–21.

Posted by: Nicole

I am really worried about my friend. She has been so depressed lately. She doesn't eat lunch at school anymore and looks so pale. I don't think she is anorexic or anything like that, but she won't tell me what's wrong! How can I find out what's wrong without being too obvious? (She hates when we ask her what's wrong.)

Should I just leave her alone? Or should I keep trying to find out? Could you please pray for her to open up and let someone know what's wrong?! How should I deal with this????

Dear Nicole,

It definitely sounds like something is wrong with your friend, but if she won't tell you what it is, there isn't much you can do. Talk to a teacher or counselor. If they don't think it is a concern continue to talk to adults that can help until one will do something. If her depression is affecting her physically then it could be a bigger issue than just usual teenage girl stuff. Remember that you do have the most powerful Person in the world to go to in Jesus. Talk to Him about her a lot. Don't pester her, but tell her that if she ever decides to unload, you are there for her and will never judge her or condemn her for whatever it is. A lot of times friends are afraid to say what's wrong because they are afraid of being judged. Show her by your daily actions and words that you don't judge people, but that you love them no matter what, just like Jesus. I am praying for your strength of spirit and wisdom in this matter. Keep up the fight for her!

Read Romans 8:26–28 and be encouraged!

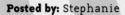

Subj: Did God talk to me?

Dear Stephanie,

The whole God-talking-to-you thing is tricky. Lots of people make it sound so easy, but it really isn't. It takes patience and testing. That's why Paul tells us to test all spirits with these four things: Scripture, wise council, circumstances, and the Holy Spirit.

Trust God to bring you the guy in His time. And believe me, His time won't be when you are obsessed with the guy. He wants you to be obsessed with Him, not a man. Until you can turn your focus toward God and away from finding love on earth, I think He will have you wait for Mr. Right.

Keep seeking Him. He has words for you. He wants you to listen intently at His feet. Put all your focus on Him and He will give you the desires of your heart.

Check out Jeremiah 10:23!

Posted by: Lindsey
At the end of every church service my pastor asks that if you aren't saved that you just raise your hand in the air and ask the Lord to come into your heart and He will. I've never done that . . . but I have, in the privacy of my own room, asked the Lord to save me. Does it still count?

Dear Lindsey,

Yes, it counts. The Father knows your heart, whether you are in church, in bed, or at school. He is the one you seek and the one you prove yourself to. Now, that doesn't discount church. The reason we go forward in church, or raise our hand, is to confirm our faith to ourselves and others. See, it's a lot easier to say "yes, I believe in God" alone in your own home than it is to stand up and admit it in front of others. It's a public claim of faith—hard to do, but totally worth the reward.

Read Matthew 3:13–17 and Titus 3:4–7.

Posted by: Heidi
My cousin who sexually abused me when I was younger is going to be moving in my house. I tried talking to Mom and Dad, but they will not listen. I am scared and not sure what to do about it.

Dear Heidi,

I am proud of you for speaking up; that's the first step in confronting evil like this. What you need to do is keep telling your parents. Also, tell other people in authority— counselor, teacher, police, principal, parents of friends— whomever you can find. I am sorry your parents don't believe you but you have to be strong and take heart that God hears you. He also asks us to take precautions to guard ourselves. Don't *ever* be alone with this person. Stay with friends if necessary 'till he is gone.

If you live in the States, call Child Help at 1-800-422-4453. They can give you more help. If you live outside the USA talk to child protective services, the police, whomever you can find. This was not your fault, take heart! You are brave and you need not stand for it. Don't give up the fight. Don't make anything easy for him. Protect yourself, and be loud if he approaches you improperly. You have nothing to be ashamed up. You are white as snow, thanks to the Father. There is healing for you, but seek help fast! Our prayers are with you.

Look at John 16:33 for courage.

Ask **Hayley**   19

Posted by: Maryanne

A lot of my friends are unintentionally influencing me in not-so-good ways. They don't mean to.

But what I mean is when I'm hanging out with some of my friends, I find myself acting differently, in ways that I know don't please God. Please pray for me, and tell me what you think?

Dear Maryanne,

It's cool you have so many friends who aren't believers; that's how we are to be the salt and light. But if the majority of your time is spent with people who don't believe what you do then you run a huge risk of crossing over slowly to what they believe, and that's not cool. I know you love these people and you should continue to do so, but you need to find a solid base of two or three believers whom you can spend the majority of your time with.

Jesus spent a lot of His time with the masses, but remember that He kept twelve believing men with Him almost all the time, and three of them really close with Him. He is our model. You will become like the people you spend most of your time with, just like you will become what you spend most of your time thinking about. Do you want to be more like Christ? Then find people who are heading in that direction.

Check out James 1:2–8, and 1 John 2:15–17. My prayers are with you. Be encouraged!

Subj: friendship is harder than it looks

Posted by: Nicole
In school, I have three friends I always hang out with. I am really close with one, and the others I am not so close to. It's really hard on me because the two friends I am not so close to sometimes pull me and my really close friend apart on purpose. One is always linking arms with me and walking off! The other is always linking arms with my close friend and walking off! But now my close friend thinks I am avoiding her but I'm not! I don't want to tell my friends to stop separating us because I am afraid I will hurt their feelings. What should I do!?

Dear Nicole,

It gets really hard when we try to act based on what people will think and not on what is right. Doing what is right, just because it is right and not because it's cool or popular is called having values. If you value honoring God over people then you can feel confident when you do what is right even if it makes people mad. It is your responsibility to be holy, not to keep your friends from being hurt. Tell your friends that it is unkind to separate you and you won't go with them next time they try. If they get mad then let them deal with it. Their feelings aren't your responsibility, honoring God is. Be faithful and He will be faithful. Don't let your friends bully you into behaving badly. Stand strong! He has given you the strength.

"Do you think I am trying to make people accept me? No, God is the One I am trying to please" (Galatians 1:10).

Posted by: Miranda

I need some help. This girl from church told me that she was in love, yes, *in love* with one of her female teachers. This girl is 14 years old. She is supposedly going out with some senior guy. Anyhow . . . she told me that about her teacher. I told her that it's just a phase she is going through and so she proceeded to full on swear at me!!! All this from a girl who says she's a Christian. I just need some advice on what I should say to her if I get to speak to her again.

Dear Miranda,

This is a really tough situation for you to be in. You've got to remember one thing though: It's the Holy Spirit's job to convict her and teach her. Your job is to show this girl the love of God. How? Stay her friend. Let her know how you feel about the situation—that you think she's going against what it says in the Bible about honoring God. But let her know that you're there if she needs to talk about things, if she needs your prayer, stuff like that. She's at a place right now where she needs support and advice. Let's make sure she's getting it from the right sources.

Prayer changes things. It can move mountains. It can radically alter lives. Just make sure you remember who God is and that you're not Him.

Check out James 1:12!

Subj: anxiety

Posted by: Lynns

I have this anxiety inside that won't go away. My mind is at a constant worry about things that I know are deceptions from the devil. I just want peace and I pray for it, but once I feel like I'm at peace it starts up again. Do you have any idea what this may be? I love Jesus, but I feel like I try to be perfect and it makes me worry about the littlest things.

Dear Lynns,

Anxiety can be a super hard thing, but it is something that we can get control of. It is also an emotion that God has given us for protection. So don't fear it, but do try to find an answer.

I encourage you to spend at least one day a week alone with God, seeking Him, thinking about Him, imagining Him, listening for Him. Let the Holy Spirit show you in your imagination what it is that Jesus can heal in you. If you have one particular thing that makes you anxious, visualize it, and then see Jesus there with you. Talk to Him and let Him talk to you. Invite him into the place and let Him clean up.

If you haven't read *Hinds Feet on High Places* by Hannah Hurnard then I would suggest it as a good walk through anxiety. Or check out *The Christian's Secret of a Happy Life* by Hannah Whitehall Smith; it is an amazing book for stress.

Sometimes anxiety can be caused by a physical condition like hormones or non-activity. Talk to a nurse or doctor about your condition too. Attack it from all angles. It cannot win. It will not. I promise you, you will be victorious.

Read Psalm 18 and Philippians 4:6–7 as your victory chants!

Ask **Hayley**

23

Posted by: Rach

I have a friend who says that she is a witch. I'm trying to talk to her about it and say what I think about it but it's hard. She says that she is a good witch and just uses her own energy to cast spells. I'm really worried about her and know she is going against God. Please help. What can I say to her?

Dear Rach,

When people are happy in the faith they have chosen and have no concern for your disagreement with it, you have to remember that it isn't your job to prove them wrong. What is your job is to introduce them to Jesus. He'll take it from there.

She's gone to the mystery of darkness because it is appealing to her craving for spiritual depth and mystery. I'd talk to her about the blood Jesus poured out for her. Of its cleansing ability and amazing power. We have powers too. They come from the Creator of good, the Author of love. And they are much more powerful than hers are.

Perhaps you could give her Frank Peretti's *This Present Darkness*. It would give her a glimpse of the reality of the spirit world and might start a good spiritual conversation. And most of all, remember to put on the armor of God. Pray for her daily, for her salvation, her healing, and her future. God will change her heart.

Check out Hebrews 12:3.

24   *Ask* **Hayley**

Posted by: giggles

How modest do you think people should dress? How do you determine what is modest or not?

Dear Giggles,

The big thing to remember is that what you show by how you dress is what guys think of you and about you. In other words, don't advertise what's not on the menu. If you have values that restrict sex to marriage then don't go around advertising sex to guys you aren't married to. Guys are totally visual. And it's your job not to make lust easy for them.

The style right now might be "skimpy is best," but you have another code to live by if you are a Christian. Don't tempt guys where they don't need to be tempted. You can still dress totally cute, just cut down on the skin exposure. Make sure you don't advertise something that's not on the menu.

Read 1 Thessalonians 4:1–8 for more on this!

Subj: picking on Christians

Posted by: X-tremeGuro1

There is just so much pressure I don't know what to do. I go to public school and am made fun of because of my looks and beliefs. I am a Christian. I know God says to stick up for you beliefs but sometimes it's tuff. Am I alone?

Dear X-tremeGuro1,

You aren't alone in feeling like this. In fact, for centuries believers have gone through pain for their faith and had to figure out the same stuff you are. What you believe is so powerful that many will try to destroy you because they don't understand it. God wants to use this time as an opportunity to draw you closer to Him and to grow you into an amazing person. Jesus said you are blessed when you are persecuted. Why? Well, 'cause when you are persecuted you are weak and you run straight to God for help. Your troubles keep you close to Him. That's way cool. If you didn't have any problems then you wouldn't need God, would you?

Check out the life of Paul. Boy did he go through hell on earth. But he didn't let that get him down. In fact, it totally stoked him up. He knew that in the adventure of life the hardest part was the best part. So do a Bible study on Paul. Get excited from the challenges God thinks you are worthy of. And let them grow you to completeness. You are very special.

"Do not be fooled: 'Bad friends will ruin good habits'" (1 Corinthians 15:33).

Posted by: Beth

My best friend died a couple of months back. She was only 18 and not a Christian. I'm still struggling with it and am drifting further and further from God. Help!!

Dear Beth,

You are going through the grieving process. It's normal to be mad when someone you love dies. You need to talk to a grief counselor to help you through this time. You can't do it on your own, God doesn't want you to. God is your refuge and strength. He is there for you to run to and He provides other people to be His arms around you. Let God use this horrible thing as a tool to make you into who you are meant to be. You have a purpose in life. What is He showing you through this? Can you help others to know Him? Can you tell more people so they can be assured of eternal life with Him?

Stay in the Word. Don't stop reading Scripture. Find worship music to listen to. Take it from Job, worship Him even when you don't feel like it, even when you are mad at Him (Job 13:15). He will lift you up and provide you with comfort. Trust that or trust nothing. The choice is yours. Read Psalm 23 for comfort.

Posted by: Biblegirl

A member of my family recently molested me; he only groped me, but that was too much. I am very confused. I think it's my fault and I am thinking about killing myself. I need all the help I can get.

Dear Biblegirl,

It is not your fault. Please find someone to tell. You need to talk to a counselor or pastor. Don't buy the lie that you can't do anything and the only solution is death. Satan will have won. Take back your life. Don't give it to the enemy. What people do to your body cannot destroy your spirit. You are strong enough to endure this pain. Just like Paul who said he was beaten but not killed, sorrowful yet always rejoicing. Many before you have suffered greatly and overcome. You can do the same.

God has an amazing way of using our suffering to make us stronger. When you get through this you will be an incredibly strong young woman. It might not seem like it now, but suffering requires perseverance. Are you ready for the challenge? God believes you are. Cling to Him and He will see you through. Don't despise your life; this episode does not define you. Forgive the man. Move beyond this and be who God created you to be.

Check out 2 Corinthians 6:9-10 for more!

Posted by: Rose

What about replacement curse words? My church and my parents don't believe in saying "Gosh, darn, or dang." They say these words actually mean just the same as saying God's name in vain or swear words. I cussed for a while, and to stop I say those words instead. Is that wrong?

Dear Rose,

There is no list of cuss words in the Bible. God wants us to talk nicely to one another, to say stuff that builds people up, not tears them down. The motive behind most cuss words is to tear people down. And that is not godly. But we can't really make a list of words and say those words are bad—it's really about the motive and how the hearer will react.

But for you, your rules are clear. They are laid out by your parents. And you are to honor your parents. So if they think euphemisms are wrong then you have to stop using them.

Once you are living on your own, you can make decisions on language based on your relationship with God. But if you decide that it's okay to hurt others with your words then you are way off. If you choose to only use words that won't hurt others then you will be doing very well.

"Honor your father and mother" (Exodus 20:12).

Posted by: Sparkle4Jesus
How much makeup should a tweener be allowed to wear?

Dear Sparkle4Jesus,

I have a question for you first. Why do you want to wear makeup? This will determine how much you should wear. If you want to do it to look older, to get more guys, or to fit in, then you should wear no makeup. If you want to do it to cover up some acne or to make yourself feel pretty, then I suggest you try a little powder and some light mascara.

The final question is: What do your parents think? This is where you have to start. They make the rules about this kind of stuff and you are called to honor them. So talk to them about it and then decide powder or no powder.

"Charm can fool you and beauty can trick you, but a woman who respects the Lord should be praised" (Proverbs 31:30).

Posted by: Blink199

I know that gossiping is wrong, but when I'm with my friends it just seems like what we do. Can I just hang out with them without actually participating in the gossip?

Dear Blink,

No, you can't hang out and just listen. Gossiping takes two people. The talker and the listener. If you are the listener you are a part of the gossip. The Bible is majorly clear on talking about people. It isn't cool. Gossip ruins friendships and makes you a fool, an idiot, a jerk. Gossip bites because it hurts the people you are talking about. Here's what I suggest you do next time your buds start to gossip. Tell them you totally have a problem with gossip and have made a decision to be holy and stop gossiping. Tell them you can't listen and you gotta go. And just get out. Don't take part. It will be totally hard. You will want to stay, as the Bible says, it tastes so good. But you have to walk away.

Proverbs 10:18; 11:13; 17:4; 18:8; 20:19—check 'em out.

Posted by: LisaLisa

My two best friends in the world are in a fight and I don't know what to do. Should I try to help them work it out? Each time I do they just end up screaming at me. But isn't that my responsibility as a friend?

Dear Lisa,

"He who passes by and meddles in a quarrel not his own is like one who takes a dog by the ear." He's stupid. He'll get bit. So here's what you do. Stay out of it. Tell them you love them both so you won't get involved. Don't be the go-between person. Don't pass on insults from them. Don't take sides. Just keep your mouth shut and tell them to work it out themselves. It doesn't involve you. They have to be grown up enough to work out their own stuff. Don't try to play God by fixing everything for everyone. Each one has to work out his life.

Proverbs 26:17 is for you.

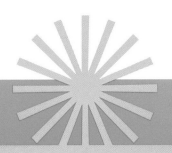

Posted by: spaceygirl
I sometimes like to read my horoscope in magazines. They are so right on most of the time. What's wrong with learning about my future?

Dear spaceygirl,
Astrology is totally condemned in Scripture. It's using something good, like the stars and planets, to manipulate people by giving them false ideas about their future. Astronomy isn't bad, but predicting what God will allow to happen is. Check out Isaiah 47:13–15. He says the astrologers are "like kindling; the fire consumes them. They can't even save themselves," so how can they save you? If you want more, get the book *Extreme A–Z* and look up all the other times the Bible talks about astrology. Check out Deuteronomy 4:19; 17:2–3; 18:10.

Posted by: Nicole
I am on a spiritual high right now. I don't want to fall into a valley. What are some things I can do to keep my walk with the Lord awesome and fired up?

Dear Nicole,
Spiritual highs are awesome, but we can't rely on them or hope to ride them forever. Enjoy every minute of it for what it is, skin on skin with the Father. Enjoy your time with Him and His gifts to you. Don't try to worry about when it will wear off, that's not your job to decide. God will move you through valleys and mountains at His pace. And each of them will be amazing, even when they don't feel like it.

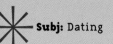
Posted by: Jazmin

I have a question 'bout dating. If I'm going out with a guy, is it bad to make out with him? In other words, is making out a sin?

Dear Jazmin,

That's a really good question. There is no place in the Bible where I can direct you to read "making out is a sin." But there are places where you can go to read about not letting there be "a hint of sexual immorality." Making out is a really dangerous thing. See it was made as the intro to sex. So even though you aren't planning on going all the way in your head, your body is totally getting ready for it. This makes it really dangerous cuz it's so hard to stop once you get rolling. And the thing about it is that once you do one thing, after awhile you get used to it and want to try something else, and that just keeps on going 'til all you have left is sex itself.

The other problem with making out is that it causes guys to have all kinds of ideas about sex. They are so much more sexual than we are usually, and so when we make out with them we make it very easy for them to sin. Jesus said that even thinking about sleeping with someone is the same as sleeping with them. EEK!! So your best bet is to avoid heavy make-out sessions 'til you are married. It will be so much better then and you won't have to feel any guilt.

Matthew 5:27–28 will help you more.

Posted by: Lauren

I have a question. When you're in a big fight with a friend what do you do? You want to be mad, but you don't want to upset God. But of course, you don't know if your friend really cares. So, what do you do?

Dear Lauren,

I always go to this verse when my friends tick me off. "A friend loves at all times and a brother is born for adversity" (Proverbs 17:17). No matter how mad you are at a friend, you have to love them. Whether they care or not, you have to love them. What good are you if you only love those who are sweet to you? Even evil people do that. The best thing you can do is what Scripture calls you to do. Time and again God calls us to be the big people. Forget about how you "feel." Live by faith, not feeling. If your friend won't work things out, you have done what God called you to do. Give her time to cool off. She'll get over it. And if she doesn't then she's not a very good friend to have around.

"So when you offer your gift to God at the altar, and you remember that your brother or sister has something against you, leave your gift there at the altar. Go and make peace with that person, then come and offer your gift" (Matthew 5:23–24).

Posted by: Eve
Does the Bible say anything about dating?

Dear Eve,
Nope. The Bible does not talk about dating. Dating is a kinda new concept. In Bible days no one would have even thought of dating. Your parents chose your husband or wife for you back then. Since relationships were about serving God and not having a crush or lusting after someone, this made total sense.

Nowadays people are a lot more concerned about being happy and finding the love of their life. This isn't bad, it's just not something that the people in Bible times were concerned about.

Posted by: Eleanor

My friend thinks she is fat but she isn't. She stopped eating, so she lost 25 lbs in like one or two months. She was in an eating disorder hospital for about two weeks but now she is out. She was doing great for awhile, but now she lost weight again (she weighs 93 lbs) and is depressed and everything. She might have to go back to the hospital and get tubes and stuff. She is being restricted from a lot of things like our middle school retreat. Her life is really messed up and her family isn't getting along. What can I do?

Dear Eleanor,

Pray. Pray for her a whole bunch. Pray with her. Pray over her. Pray with friends. Pray, pray, pray.

And read Philippians 4:6–7.

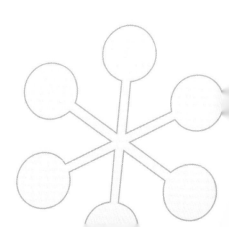

Subj.: bad friends

Posted by: Kayla88

I'm 14 and my life is so hard right now. I go to a Christian school, and 2 of my friends from that school are basically having sex. They are both questioning their faith in God. I actually prayed with and encouraged them to accept Christ, BUT IT JUST FEELS LIKE THEY PULLED OUT MY HEART AND STOMPED ON IT. Sometimes it feels like it's my fault they might be giving up on God, because I can't answer their questions or wasn't helping them enough. I'm just overwhelmed. Help!

Dear Kayla88,

Take a break from playing God. God would love to do that job if you would just let Him. Trust Him to take care of all your friends. Remember, He asks us to live in peace, not in stress.

Your friend's salvation, hopes, problems—none of them are your responsibility. What is your responsibility is to pray for them and leave them with Him.

Take your eyes off the creation and put them back onto the Creator. He will guide you and your friends. Just trust Him.

"Do not worry about anything, but pray and ask God for everything you need, always giving thanks. And God's peace, which is so great we cannot understand it, will keep your hearts and minds in Christ Jesus" (Philippians 4:6–7).

Ask **Hayley**

Posted by: Mikey

I really, really want to get a tattoo, but what does the Bible say about them? Is it against God?

Dear Mikey,

In the Old Testament law tattoos were forbidden. But when Christ came, He redeemed us from the curse of the law (Galatians 3). This means that God looks at your heart, your motives, when it comes to what you do.

Why do you want a tattoo? To get attention? To be cool? Check your motives, are they holy? That's all God asks.

"Everything is permissible, but not everything is beneficial" (1 Corinthians 10:23).

"You shall not make any cuttings in your flesh for the dead, nor tattoo any marks on you, for I am the Lord" (Leviticus 19:28).

Posted by: cole-lee

I'm having a hard time with my boyfriend trying to figure out what God wants us to do with our relationship. He's into the thing where we have absolutely no physical relationship. While I agree with his reasoning, I have no idea what God thinks about a physical relationship—kissing, hand-holding . . . nothing bad or anything. We don't call our relationship "dating" or "going out" because we feel that most people our age do not remain together. Also, we feel that the pressures one gets from others when in the shadow of those titles are bad. I just need help. I've consulted the Bible numerous times, but am not having luck finding relationship advice.

Dear Cole-lee,

The Bible doesn't really talk about dating because people in those times didn't date. Most marriages were arranged. For solid Christian advice you can check out a couple of books. Joshua Harris has a book called *I Kissed Dating Goodbye*. This sounds like it goes along with what your boyfriend is feeling. On the other side of the spectrum, there's *I Gave Dating a Chance* by Jeramy Clark. Then there's *Dateable*, one I'd highly recommend, by author Justin Lookadoo. In it he describes how to have great character while dating. He gives really practical advice on relationships.

Also, take a look at these verses on what it means to honor God: 2 Corinthians 9–10; 1 Peter 1:15–16.

Ask **Hayley**

41

Subj: Sex on the mind

Posted by: Thomas
Is something wrong with me? All I think about is sex. I'm only 13. Help!

Dear Thomas,
No, nothing is wrong with you. Your hormones are just starting to kick in. That's a wild ride, and part of it is that sex is always on your mind. Don't feel like a freak, cuz you're just normal.

But don't make it worse by fantasizing and thinking of ways to act on it. When the thoughts come, know they are just human, and go on with your life. You can control your thoughts by not spending hours dreaming about them. Stay in control and you will be fine.

Check out what Philippians 4:8–10 has to say.

Posted: Dana

I love Jesus—the only problem is with my dad! I've always wanted to go to church to learn more about the Lord, but my dad always steps in our way. My mother, my sister and I are always looking around for the right church to go to. But my dad doesn't want us to go. Instead of going to church, I've been reading 2 chapters of the Bible every night. Is this enough?

Dear Dana,

It's tough when someone else controls your life, but 'til you are eighteen you are kind of stuck. God sees your problem and understands, so yes, do your Bible study as much as you can. But how about this: Look at school and see if there are any Christian clubs. Get your mom and sister together to do a Bible study once a week with you. You guys could even do worship there at home with a CD. Your dad might even start to see the relationship side of God as you all worship Him. Most of all pray, pray, pray. Ask God to speak to your dad. Remember, God thinks you are worthy of this trial or He wouldn't have allowed it to happen to you. Be faithful.

Posted by: Angel

I made a commitment not to date in high school a couple of months ago. Well, I've started going to this new youth group with my buddy Jodie from a retreat. There're these two guys, Alex and Matt, and they're so hilarious. Jodie's kinda got a thing for Alex, and she's even taking him to prom. Matt's just totally confusing to me. The first time I met him was when we went ice skating, and he ended up sitting on my lap on the ride back cuz there wasn't enough seats for everyone. I barely know him, but I can't stop thinking about him! It's insane. Jodie wants the four of us (Alex, Matt, her, and me) to go on a "double friend-ing" (since I'm not dating). I really want to go, but I'm not sure if it's alright for me to. What do you think?

Dear Angel,

Here's the deal, once you make a commitment to something the enemy will try to pull you away from it. You lack will, faith and devotion if at the first temptation you cave from your commitment. I'm not saying dating is bad, but since you committed not to, you have to stick with your commitment. (But "friending" is just a way of getting away with dating by calling it something else.)

God is watching, and he says "If I can't trust you with the small things, like this, why will I ever trust you with bigger things?" My advice, stick out your commitment. I know it's hard but hard stuff builds perseverance, and perseverance character. God is testing you; will you pass?

Read Luke 16:10–11.

Posted by: best friend
Help!! This girl I've known since kindergarten was once the girl I called my best friend. Ever since the 8th grade she's been hooked on bowling. And now she has become more attached to it as we venture on our way as sophomores in high school. She bowls with a league and she does it every weekend and sometimes throughout the week. Not only do I not like bowling, but I can see her putting it before God. I've tried to bring her close to God and get her involved in church, but she won't listen. We never do anything together anymore because she blows all our plans for bowling. What should I do??

Dear best friend,

Have you explained to your friend how you feel? Right now all she might be hearing is you trying to **change** her. Maybe if she just heard that you really like her and really miss her she would be more open to your feelings. You might want to take up bowling. You could spend time with her and have ops to talk about God in her world. It's a lot easier to **show** someone the love of God than it is to **tell** them about the love of God. God wants you to live at peace, knowing full well that He is in control. All He asks is that you control yourself, not others. What he asks you to do is to love them. She's already heard all about God, now show Him to her. Love her. Love her hard, love her long and love her good. Scripture says friends are made for adversity. Don't run cuz the going gets tough. Stick it out. You are a faithful friend.

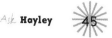

Posted by: Beth

Found a quote in the Bible the other day that said that anyone who sins against God or Jesus will be forgiven, but anyone who sins against the Holy Spirit won't be. Can anyone explain the meaning of this? What if I have committed the unforgivable sin? What will happen? In one way I'm worried that I may have committed the unforgivable sin when I wasn't a Christian, and so can't be forgiven. What do you think?

Dear Beth,

"So I tell you, people can be forgiven for every sin and everything they say against God. But whoever speaks against the Holy Spirit will not be forgiven. Anyone who speaks against the Son of Man can be forgiven, but anyone who speaks against the Holy Spirit will not be forgiven, now or in the future" (Matthew 12:31–32).

Subj: veggies

Posted by: Curious
Is Jesus a vegetarian? For instance I know he ate fish and bread a lot, but did he ever eat meat??

Dear Curious,

Jesus would have followed a Kosher diet. He was Jewish and ate many of his meals at Jewish homes. This means the diet was high in fish and grains. But he also would have eaten meat occasionally such as cow, considered a clean animal, and lamb. Beef was harder to come by, so it was served only on special occasions, such as feasts. Lamb and goat were more abundant, so the Jews ate mostly that meat. Pork was not eaten. Jesus also would have eaten eggs and clean poultry, as well as butter, milk products and vegetables. Jesus would have eaten what the people were eating.

Check out Leviticus 7:23-27; 11:12-19; 14:11-17; and Numbers 14:20.

Posted by: level-headed
Is it ever ok to litter? I mean aren't we going overboard
with this whole save the planet thing?

Dear level-headed,

There is no question that some people go overboard on the
save the planet thing when they value the lives of animals
above the lives of people. But being concerned for our
planet is not a radical stance to take. God gave us dominion
over the earth and animals and that means that he trusts it
all to our care. There are really two issues. One is honoring
God and that which he has given us to protect. The other is
that littering is against the law. And we are asked to obey
the law even if we don't agree with it. So if you want to
honor God then respect the planet.

Dear Worried,

Two answers. Yes and no. On God's scale of sin, all sins are all wrong and therefore all just as miserable as the next. BUT, on a human scale there are definitely worse sins than others. To murder your friend is much, much worse than to gossip about her. True, they each show the sin of your heart, but murdering her is horrific.

The problem with thinking that some sins are worse than others is that we put them on a scale and decide that anything below 5 is OK for us to do. That's not true. So look at all sin as an abomination to God, but know that according to the police and other people in authority some stuff has worse consequences than others.

Subj: Psychic

Posted by: Tooly5
I'm dying to find out about my future. Is it ok if I just go to a psychic to see what she has to say?

Dear Tooly,

Nope. It isn't okay if you just go to check it out. It isn't okay to play at that kind of stuff. God is very strict about it. He says that "the person who turns after mediums and familiar spirits (psychics, fortune-tellers, witches, channelers) to prostitute himself with them, I will set My face against that person and cut him off from his people." Ouch! Sounds serious. It is. God says if you go to these kind of people for direction you will become His enemy. Not a good thing to be.

So here's what I suggest. You have options. You have ways of knowing what to do with your life. The Holy Spirit will talk to you if you will listen; find a place to be silent. Give Him time to talk. Slow down and look for Him, listen for Him. Check out the Bible for the stuff you are wanting answers to. God can totally speak through the words. If you have trouble finding stuff get a concordance like *Extreme A-Z* and look stuff up there. Don't settle for a cheap imitation (fortune-teller) when you have the real thing right with you (God). Remember, "Greater is He who is in you than he who is in the world." He's the one with all the truth. Not them.

Check out 2 Kings 17:17-18, 1 Chronicles 10:13, and Ezekiel 13:20-23 for more on fortune-tellers.

50   *Ask* **Hayley**

Posted by: Marcus

My teacher says that the God that Jews and Muslims and all other religions worship is the same as our God. She says there is only one God, and that's from the Bible. Is that true?

Dear Marcus,

It's true that there is only one God. But that doesn't mean that the God that other religions worship is the same God. There are lots of gods, small 'g.' These are substitutes for the real God. Kind of like the idols you read about in the Bible.

But when it comes to the big God, the one and only God, He isn't the same in all religions. Check out what the gods in other religions say, and you'll see they have completely different personalities than our God—they can't be the same entity. The Jews do worship the God found in the Old Testament of the Bible, but they reject Jesus Christ as the Son of God. They say things that completely contradict our God. So no, we don't all worship the same God.

" . . . God is the only Lord and there is no other God besides him" (Mark 12:23b).

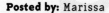

Subj: Meditation

Posted by: Marissa

I want to meditate, but my parents aren't sure it's OK. Is it ok for Christians to mediate?

Dear Marissa,

Meditation is a Christian discipline that has been taken on by other non-Christian traditions and changed to something that God isn't involved in. But in real Christian meditation, God is very involved. All over the Psalms it tells us to meditate on God's Word. Tell your parents that you are meditating on God, His Word and His person. See what they say.

There are several really good books on the subject. Richard Foster wrote *A Celebration of Discipline*, a classic work on the spiritual life where he teaches you about meditation. And Thomas Merton wrote *Thoughts in Solitude*, which also teaches you how to meditate on God. Meditation is nothing to be afraid of if God is at the center of it. In fact, it is called for in Scripture.

For more on that you can go to: Psalm 1:2; 4:4; 16:7; 19:14; 119:15; Matthew 6:5,6; 2 Timothy 2:7; Hebrews 3:1.

Posted by: Kaila67

I have a confession. I totally hate my brother. I mean I really hate him. I wish he were never born. How can God expect me to love someone who can be such a jerk?

Dear Kaila,

Brothers can be total jerks and impossible to love, but yep, God does expect you to love him. How holy would you be if you only loved people who were easy to love? But check it, love doesn't have to feel good. You don't have to feel like you love him, you only have to act like it. In fact, you don't even have to like him. But God knows your brother and knew he would be your brother long before he ever was. What does God want you to learn by having him around? It might just be that God wants you to learn that love isn't a feeling but a decision. If you want to be holy you have to practice loving the unlovable. And your brother is the perfect place to start. After all, you wouldn't be any better than evil people if you only loved people who made you feel good.

Check out 1 Corinthians 13. Learn what love really means. It isn't always fun.

Subj: old sins

Posted by: TreyW23
When I was younger I did some really bad stuff. Now that I am a Christian I still can't forgive myself. Can God forgive me even if I can't?

Dear Trey,

Yes, that's why He's God and we aren't. God has a totally cool ability to forgive the worst sins in the world. That's what the whole Christ dying on the cross for all the sins of the world was about. He did that just so your horrible sin could be forgiven. So even though you can't do it, He can. All you need to do is confess what you did to him and then believe Him to forgive. But if that still isn't working, I would suggest this: find a pastor who you trust who you can confess to. Tell him your problem of not being able to forgive yourself and ask if he will let you tell him what you've done. Then write down on a sheet of paper all the horrible junk you have done. Don't leave any of it off. Then go in and tell them to him. When you are done he will tell you that God forgives you for all of that. He will confer God's blessing and forgiveness on you. The Bible tells us to confess our sins one to another. People serve as the voice of God in our lives. God did that on purpose. Allow someone to offer you God's forgiveness. It will change your whole life.

Read Nehemiah 9:17, Psalm 86:5, and Acts 13:38–39.

Posted by: 77Birdie88

My parents are getting divorced and I am worried. Will God hate them if they get married again because he hates divorce?

Dear Birdie,

It's true, the Bible does say that God hates divorce. Just like he hates gossip, lying, murder, pride and all other sins. That doesn't mean he hates the person who commits the sin. If that were the case, He would hate all of us. God will still love your parents after the divorce, but that doesn't mean He won't discipline them. All things we do that are against God's law have outcomes. That is God's discipline on the people that He loves. So this means they will probably be really sad and feel pretty bad for awhile.

They will have to work through it with God.

For more info on divorce look at Mathew 19:3; Romans 7:1-3; 1 Corinthians 7:10-11.

Subj: My dad's going to hell

Posted by: Tiff219

My Dad says he believes in God, but he won't go to church with us. My Mom tells him he's going to hell. That scares me. Is he really going to hell?

Dear Tiff,

Not for not going to church. People are saved by faith, not by works. Your Mom is probably more concerned that your Dad doesn't really know God. Going to church might be the only way she thinks he will come to know Him. Maybe it's time for a family meeting. See if they will all sit down and talk it out. Does your Dad understand salvation? Does He love God? And can your Mom live with His decision? Cuz she can't harass him into salvation. She can only do it by loving him.

If your Dad doesn't understand who Christ is, maybe you can help him. But don't push Him on him, love him in Him. Church is a place all believers should be going, but not going doesn't send you to hell.

Check out Ephesians 2:8 to see how people are saved by grace.

Posted by: Stacielu
My dog died last week and I've been so depressed since then. I have to know—do animals have souls?

Hey Stacie,

The Bible doesn't say anything about animals having souls, but that doesn't mean that God doesn't care for them and protect them and maybe even take them to heaven. Animals don't have souls, which means they don't have free will in the way that we do. They don't choose evil or good, God or no God. They just live by the instinct God gave them. We can't know for sure if they go to heaven, because the Bible doesn't ever say, but we can know that God loves them and created them for us. Trust God with their death just like you trust Him with your life.

"Good people take care of their animals . . ." (Proverbs 12:10).

Posted by: 3agape3
Are there really angels like in *Touched by an Angel* that we can see and talk to?

Dear Agape,
In the Bible angels talked to people all the time. They sometimes appeared looking like normal people, sometimes not. *TBAA* tries to show that by lighting Monica differently when she says she is an angel, giving her an angelic aura. But angels were always helping people in Scripture—like the ones who went to tell Lot about Sodom and Gomorrah, the one who came to Mary, and the ones who Elijah saw surrounding him and the enemy. Paul tells us to be kind to everyone cuz you never know when you are talking to an angel.

But to be obsessed about finding or seeing angels is not what God wants. Just know that they are there and that they are sent by God. Love people and don't expect anything from them like they are angels. Just love them because God loves you.
Check out Hebrews 1:13–14 and Hebrews 13:1–2.

Posted by: Jen12
Do people become either ghosts or angels when they die?

Dear Jen,
Angels are not dead people. Once people die they either go
to heaven or to hell. They don't come back to earth to talk
to their friends and guide them like lots of movies pretend
they do. God created angels before He created man. Angels
were made to work for God. They ran errands for Him, like
coming to earth to tell a little girl that she was going to
give birth to Christ. They were also made to protect us.
Ghosts aren't mentioned in Scripture. But what *is*
mentioned are the demons who came down here with
Satan. Satan was an angel gone bad. The demons function
like ghosts in stuff like spiritual warfare. They are evil and
want to beat the children of God in the war for souls.

"Why are people important to you? . . . You made them a little
lower than the angels and crowned them with glory and honor. You
put all things under their control" (Hebrews 2:6–7).

Posted by: Helena

My friend believes in aliens. She is totally convinced they exist. What does the Bible say about aliens? How do I talk to her about them?

Dear Helena,

The Bible doesn't say anything about aliens. Some think that means there aren't any. Some would say the ones people see are only demons. Others say that they are really aliens. If God can make people on this planet, there is no reason to think He couldn't make them on other planets and in other galaxies. There is something that Paul said about being a Christian. He said not to concern yourself with civilian matters. You are a soldier and you need to keep the main thing the main thing. There might be aliens. We don't know. And frankly it doesn't matter. What matters is that we love God and love our neighbors and that we tell others about Him.

Don't start arguments about little things that make no difference in your relationship with others. Just don't even concern yourself with it. They might exist, they might not; that doesn't affect your relationship with Christ or His love for the people of this earth.

"Now I know only a part, but then I will know fully, as God has known me" (1 Corinthians 13:12).

Posted by: Bobby32
Does God really know everything?

Dear Bobby,
Yep. He knows everything.
Check out Psalm 139, Hebrews 4:13, and Isaiah 46:9–10.

Posted by: kristin1983

Do you have any opinions on whether Christians should be in chatrooms? In the worldly ones cybering is rampant and the "Christian" ones I've been in aren't much better. I just think it is so easy to get sucked into them and fall.

I think they are really a problem that needs to be dealt with and I think that it is probably best for most Christians to stay out of them. What do you think?

Dear Kristin,

Scripture says everything is permissible but not everything is beneficial. This means there is no hard law about stuff like chatrooms so we have to come to our own conclusions. The last thing we should do as believers is do something that will tempt us, because once tempted sin isn't far behind. I would suggest that if anyone is weak and prone to cybering then they shouldn't go to chatrooms. It would not be beneficial. But if someone has no problem whatsoever with cybering then chatrooms can be a great place to witness.

Unfortunately, we also run the risk of spending so much time in front of a computer with people we don't really know, that we fail to live.

Everything in moderation. Get outside, make friends with people you can see, have fun, spend time in solitude, worship, study, and chat a little but don't let it become your life.

Check out 1 Corinthians 10:23-33 for more on this.

Posted by: Suzie

I have this burning desire for Jesus, and I want to get to know Him better. And I want to hear His voice. But sometimes I get frustrated because it seems like I'm not getting the response I want. My Mom just says to be patient, and there are so many times I feel like I'm just praying from my head, not my spirit. And I question a lot of things that I am for sure about in the beginning. My mind just tends to over think things. Do you have any helpful words of advice? I love Him and I want to have a sincere heart toward Him.

Dear Suzie,

Maybe you need to consider what the 'response you want' is. We love God *not* to get something out of it but because we want to *give* something to Him, our love, our worship. If you feel like you are praying with your head and not your spirit then you might be telling God what you want more than you are loving Him for who He is. Try this next time you pray: Think of Him as a friend, a really loving friend. Now imagine Him sitting by a lake. Walk up to Him and sit with him. Lean against Him. Be in His presence. Imagine His smell, his touch, his presence. What does it feel like? Use your imagination to just be with Him, no agenda, no need other than His presence.

Isaiah 55 has more to say.

Subj: Suicide

Dear JP,

If you think that someone you know has serious thoughts of suicide then you have to tell someone. A teacher, a pastor, parent, an adult who can help them. Suicide isn't the answer to your friend's problems. It only creates more problems and leaves a world of hurt behind it. The best thing you can do for your friend is get them help. After you do that your next step is prayer. Cover them in prayer for protection and insight. Find another friend to pray with. Intercede for 'em. Help them fight this battle in the spiritual realm. Let the adults help fight it in the physical.

Galatians 6:2 and 1 Thessalonians 5:17 have more to say.

Posted by: LouLou
Ever feel like God is pulling away from you? What did you do to get better?

Dear LouLou,

Many people have felt like God was pulling away from them, you aren't alone, but the thing is that God doesn't pull away from us. He is always there, but sometimes He is there in different ways. Faith isn't a feeling, and the way we feel about God shouldn't change what we believe about Him. What you are going through right now is called the desert. You are dry, bored, can't find God, wondering if He has left. That's normal. This might be your time of testing, as He tested the Israelites in the desert. Your job is to believe in Him even in this dry place. Don't budge. Don't make hasty decisions, wait for Him to reveal Himself. It may take days, it may take months, but your job is to wait and never stop believing.

Once you are through the desert you will be a stronger believer, more prepared for the battle before you. God will reveal Himself to you in His own time. Remember, He promises that if you will seek Him you will find Him. Keep seeking, don't ever give up and believe that He will show Himself eventually.

"Faith is being sure of what we hope for and certain of what we do not see" (Hebrews 11:1).

Ask **Hayley**   65

Posted by: hot for Jesus
Can people really know they're a Christian?

Dear Hot for Jesus,

Most definitely. God's Word makes it very clear. If you confess with your mouth and believe in your heart that Jesus is Lord, you will be saved. And once they've done them they can know they are Christians.

Now some people get confused and think they are Christians when they are not because they don't know this about salvation. They have been taught by someone other than God's Word and they think they are a Christian if they do this or that, or go to this church or that church. But that is not what Scripture says makes a Christian. So you may run into a lot of people who say they are Christians, but really aren't. You can never know that for sure. All you can know for sure is if you are.

Want to read more? Check out Romans 10:9, 1 John 5:11-12, and 2 Corinthians 5:17.

Posted by: ~Living4God~

I was saved when I was 11 years old and I am still. Something in my mind keeps saying I'm not saved but I know I am. What do I do or what is happening? I keep on asking God in my heart, but something keeps telling me I'm not saved. Help!

Dear Living4God,

The enemy loves to lie to us. He uses these lies to freak us out and keep us from doing anything for God and sometimes from even loving Him. There is nothing wrong with you, this happens to a lot of people. What you need to do is make it too hard and too boring for the enemy to keep bugging you about this. Here's what you do. Get some 3 x 5 note cards. Then go through your Bible and find every verse on the love of God. Write down things about what it takes to be saved. And things about how no one can take you from him.

Find all the verses you can on how much God loves you and will protect you. These are your weapons. Right now you are trying to fight a war with no weapons, and you are losing. But we can fix that. Write down each verse on its own card. Carry these with you and whenever the enemy starts lying to you say 'no' outloud and then start to read your cards. Use your weapons, lob them at him, fire them at him, throw them at him. Use them to do what they do: defeat the enemy.

Check out John 10:27–30; Romans 9:16; Ephesians 2:1–10; and Ephesians 6:1–18.

Ask **Hayley**   67

Posted by: NotAshamed4Him
How can we not be part of the world and keep ourselves holy, but at the same time show them Christ's love and light?

Dear NotAshamed4Him,

To be set apart from the world means that the world is not your first love. It means that the things of the world aren't your obsession, but God is. It means that you don't participate in the sinful activity of the world, and that you don't envy those who do.

It doesn't mean that you remove yourself from the world to protect yourself. It doesn't mean you don't love the people of this world. And it doesn't mean that you only hang out with Christians.

Christians are the light of the world, and if they don't go out and light the world it will stay dark. To hoard your light and keep it from others is selfish. You are called to love others. Paul even said that he would gladly give up his own salvation if it would save his people.

"Do not love the world or the things in the world. If you love the world, the love of the Father is not in you. These are the ways of the world: wanting the sinful things we see, and being too proud of what we have. None of these come from the Father, but all of them come from the world" (1 John 2:15–16).

Posted by: Felicity

I use to cuss pretty badly because my friends did. I don't do it near as much as I use to but every once in a while one will slip out. Any tips on how to stop completely? I REALLY want to spread God's word and be a good example, but I can't exactly do that if I'm not.

Dear Felicity,

Usually what comes out of our mouths is just the stuff that is overflowing from our heart. That is, whatever we are really feeling starts coming out in what we say. Check out your cussing, does it have to do with anger? Like do you get all mad and scream cuss words? If so then ask God to start to work on your anger. Find verses on it. Figure out why you care about things so much that it makes you mad. Or do you cuss to be cool? If so then you need to work on your heart. You are probably more concerned about pleasing your friends than God. Find verses on that.

Don't get all upset with yourself either. This might take time. If you think it hinders your witness explain to people that just because you love God it doesn't mean you are perfect. That will be a good witness for people who think they have to be perfect before God will accept them. Allow your downfalls to be things that lift others up.

Make 2 Timothy 2:16 your creed.

Posted by: neenee
I would like to know how to pray and why do you pray the way you do?

Dear Neenee,

When Jesus was asked this question he spoke the Lord's Prayer. A good way to pray is to follow His lead, not word for word, but idea for idea:

Our Father who art in heaven—acknowledge that He is God. He is the ruler of the universe.

Hallowed be thy name—glorify Him. Worship Him.

Thy kingdom come, thy will be done on earth as it is in heaven—tell Him that no matter what, you want HIS will for your life.

Give us this day our daily bread—this is where you ask him to fill your needs, remembering that He knows better than you what's the best.

And forgive us our trespasses—this is where we confess that we are messed up and that we need his forgiveness everyday.

As we forgive those who trespass against us—think of the people you are mad at. Forgive them in front of God.

And lead us not into temptation but deliver us from evil—pray for his protection on your life; pray for the armor of God (Ephesians 6).

For thine is the kingdom and the power and the glory for ever and ever—once again acknowledge that He is an amazing God.

Read the Lord's Prayer in Matthew 6:9–18.

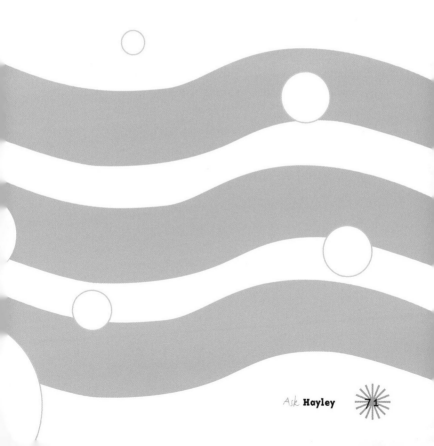

Posted by: Chris56

Why does everyone always refer to God as 'HE' ? God is neither male nor female so why don't people call God 'SHE' instead?

Dear Chris,

We refer to God as He because that is how He most often refers to himself in the Bible. God the Father has qualities that are typically thought to be masculine (like power, justice, honor, etc.) and some that are typically thought of as feminine (like nurturing, love, compassion, etc.)—but he is always described as male in the Bible.

Keep in mind, when Jesus came to earth he wasn't a girl. This is where we get our most common image of God—in the person of Jesus Christ.

"Our Father in heaven . . ." (Matthew 6:9).

Posted by: Cindy4Jesus

Hey, I've got a question. I just want to know your opinion. If you accept Christ but later you kind of turn from him, or start to go down the wrong road, does God stick with you until there is no chance of restoration? Or are you assured eternal life no matter how far you turn away from Christ or rebuke him?

Dear Cindy,

Scripture tells us that salvation has nothing to do with what we DO but what we believe, that is in God. But it also says in Romans 10:9 that we have to make Him Lord of our lives. When you make Him Lord of your life weird things start to happen (see Galatians 5:22–23). You start to change. You get better, you start to love Him more. That doesn't mean you are perfect and never sin again, but it does mean that your life looks different. Jesus said you could tell a tree by the kind of fruit it produced. We can never know if others are saved, but we can have a good idea by the kind of fruit their lives produce.

If a person claims to be saved but then acts like they are an enemy of God, despising Him, turning from Him and disobeying Him purposefully, then they probably never really made Him Lord of their life.

Study Matthew 13 and let God tell you what it all means.

Posted by: Amber

A friend of mine has it set in his mind that he wants to take the place of people that are in hell because he doesn't think he deserves being in heaven, so he wants to go to hell so everybody in hell can go to heaven in place of him. I don't know what to tell him. I tried everything.

Dear Amber,

Your friend has a God complex. God came to earth to die for everyone so they wouldn't have to go to hell. God, Jesus, did that once and for all so your friend doesn't have to.

But the bigger issue seems to be your friend's guilt. He feels really guilty for something, something so big that he thinks even God can't forgive him (if he is indeed a believer).

If he isn't a believer then you can offer him the chance to have all his sins forgiven by God. A lot of non-believers are plagued with guilt, and they don't realize that God is waiting to forgive them. All they have to do is believe that Jesus already died for the sins of the world, so they don't have to.

Share God's love with your friend. Help him find a godly man who he can shares his pains with. As a girl you can't be the one to do that. A man must speak life to a man. Pray for him and lead him to where he needs to be.

"God loved the world so much that he gave his one and only Son so that whoever believes in him may not be lost, but have eternal life" (John 3:16).

Posted by: Katie
I have a friend who has a friend who doesn't believe that once you are saved you are always saved and you don't have to keep doing it over and over again. I was wondering if you could tell me where I could find Bible reference for that.

Dear Katie,

Sure. Below are some verses you can show your friend. How fickle would God be if he forgot each day that we believed in Him and had to hear it over and over again in order to save us. When does the change happen? At midnight? As soon as you wake up? Is there a schedule for salvation? See how silly the idea is? It is a rule made up by misguided humans. Once you are somebody's child you are their child forever, and God calls us His children. It seems too easy, and it is. He loves us that much.

Check out how easy it is: Romans 5:8-11; Ephesians 2:1-22; Romans 10:9,13; Romans 8:1; Hebrews 7:25; Hebrews 10:11-18; 1 John 5:11-12; Romans 4:13-18; John 1:12.

Posted by: Vanessa
What if I doubt Jesus? I want to believe in him so bad. I want to be for sure he is real but I just can't understand.

Dear Vanessa,

It's ok to doubt, in fact it's kinda normal. But remember you are a believer, not a doubter, so by definition you must say no to the doubt and determine in your mind, set your mind, to believe him even if it seems preposterous. Remember faith is believing in things you can't see.

Do a Bible study on faith. Find every verse you can on it. Learn them. Memorize them. You don't have to feel like you believe in order to believe, just choose to. I don't believe that planes can fly, I really don't. I mean how can they? But I choose to believe that they have for years so it must work somehow.

If it helps, start by believing in small things at first. Pray to God and make a list of your prayers. Leave room to write the answers to those prayers. Watch the page fill up. But remember, you have to believe and not doubt, not feel, just believe that He will be faithful to His word.

Get with some friends who believe strongly. Learn from them. Be encouraged by them. And your faith will grow day by day.

"Abram believed the Lord. And the Lord accepted Abram's faith, and that faith made him right with God" (Genesis 15:6).

Posted by: Miranda

I'm doing an assignment at school on suicide and what effect all religions have had on it. Like how the religion has changed the person's mind about whether or not suicide is wrong. I cannot find *anything* in the Bible that says whether it is wrong or right. Plus I myself have seriously considered suicide and so I am very curious to know what God thinks of it.

Dear Miranda,

To kill yourself is not a sin punishable by hell, but it is a sin like any other. It says to God, "I am in control of my life, *not* you. You've not taken very good care of me down here and so it's over. You lose." Suicide is the ultimate act of selfishness. "I hurt. I want to relieve my pain, no matter how much it hurts others."

The people we leave behind suffer greatly from our act of suicide. Dying to self, as Christ died to self, would mean leaning into the pain, following the path God has set for us because we believe He knows the way.

So the bigger question is, are we willing to obey Scripture, to suffer along with Jesus, to be weak so He may be strong? In this world you will have troubles, but take heart He has overcome the world (Jn. 16:33).

For more info check out www.christianitytoday.com/ct/2000/127.42.0.html.

Read these verses: 1 Cor. 6:19-20; 2 Cor. 1:8-11; 2 Cor. 4:16-18; Phil. 4:4-9; Col. 3:2.

Ask **Hayley**

Subj: Divorce

Posted by: Becca
How can I deal with my parents' divorce? It is hard for me to really trust in God and I even give up on God half the time. How can I trust in God when I think that God did all of this?

Dear Becca,

I don't know why your parents have decided to get divorced, but it isn't God's idea. The Bible says, "What God has brought together let no man tear apart." It's the law and God can't and won't go against His own law. God let's us do whatever we want, but there are always consequences for ourselves and those around us.

It really sucks that your parents couldn't work it out. But you now need to figure out what God is going to teach you through this. Remember, the testing of your faith develops perseverance. And perseverance leads to perfection. If your life never has any bumps in it then you will never grow. How can you learn to trust God unless you have something you can't handle yourself? You have to trust Him now more than ever or your faith will falter. Don't let the enemy use this one battle to destroy you. You are too valuable to the kingdom for that.

"The Lord is my strength and my shield. I trust him, and he helps me. I am very happy, and I praise him with my song" (Psalm 28:7).

Posted by: Littlegurl
Does God always love me?

Dear Littlegurl,

Yes.

Read more in Ephesians 3, 1 John 3, Romans 5, and Psalm 36.

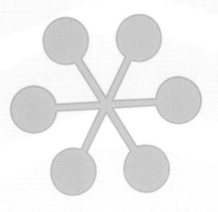

Posted by: Beth

Hey, whatdya guys think about demon possession? Can Christians be demon possessed? How dya get rid of them, if so? I have a friend who is very worried about it as she has gone from being a Satanist to a Christian. Can someone who has sold their soul to the devil be a Christian??

Dear Beth,

A better translation for most of the instances of 'demon possession' in the Bible is 'demonized.' Demons, or Satan, can only possesses you if you allow them to. That means they can't possess true Christians. But they can bother the heck out of you. A lot of people are demonized long after they get saved. This might be the case with your friend. If she gave her life to Satan, but then rebuked him and gave her life to Christ, Satan can no longer own her. But he can bother her. That is, the demons she allowed to control her could still be hanging around whispering stuff in her ear.

If she is concerned that she hasn't gotten rid of all of them, she should talk to a pastor. Confession of your sins, and the instances when you allowed demons to run your life or enter your mind, will force the demons out into the open. And they hate being out in the open. Jesus said that there are some demons who take a lot of time in prayer to get rid of. This might not be a quick fix for her. She needs to seek godly counsel and godly intercessors to help her fight the enemy that she used to befriend.

Check out Ephesians 6:10–18 to see how to protect yourself.

Posted by: Kristian

Should I be scared about God coming back?

Dear Kristian,

In the Old Testament, whenever people saw God or his angels they freaked out. But whenever anybody saw Christ they were healed, cleansed and saved. Christ will be the one who will come back for us, and believe me, you won't be scared at all. It will probably be the most amazing feeling you have ever felt in your life. He isn't coming back to judge and condemn believers, but to take us to heaven to be with God. There is nothing to fear in that. God is a lover of His children. The ones who need to be scared are the ones who don't know Him.

Read Revelation 7:9–17 to see how great it will be.

Posted by: myckie-4-christ
How was God created? How did he get here?

Dear Myckie-4-christ,

Scripture tells us that there was never a time when God wasn't. He has always existed. If He were created then He wouldn't be God. The one who created Him would be God. It's really impossible for us humans to wrap our minds around it, isn't it? That's why it takes faith. Faith is being sure of what you hope for and certain of what you do not see.

Read Hebrews 11:1 for more.

Subj: Swearing

Posted by: Kt
All of my friends swear, even Christian friends. I'm confused. Why is swearing wrong? I know that u shouldn't use God's name carelessly (if u c wot i mean) but why do people think it's so bad?

Dear Kt,

You're right, the fourth commandment says that you shall not use the name of the Lord in vain. In other words, don't use his name for a cuss word. And Scripture also says not to swear by anyone or anything. That means you shouldn't say "I swear to God" for someone to believe you. Your yes should mean yes and your no should mean no.

We can't make a list of words that are illegal and ones that are OK. What we can do is decide not to say anything that is cruel, that would hurt someone else, or that others would find offensive. Our job is to protect others. Cussing itself isn't evil, but hurting others is.

> "Let no corrupt word proceed out of your mouth, but what is good for necessary edification, that it may impart grace to the hearers" (Ephesians 4:29).

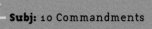

Posted by: Kristin

What does "You shall not commit adultery" mean?

Dear Kristin,

According to the American Heritage Dictionary *adultery* is "voluntary sexual intercourse between a married person and a partner other than the lawful spouse." But Jesus took this commandment a step further. He said that if you even look at someone lustfully you have committed adultery with them. That means that if you daydream all day about your friends husband, it's like you've already slept with him in your soul.

Sex is meant to be between a man and a woman who are married. Anytime you take it outside that environment you disobey God.

Read Matthew 5:27–30 to find out more.

Dear Jamie,

That means you aren't supposed to go around lying about
people. Making up stuff. Spreading rumors. Making them out
to be what they aren't. It also means not letting a rumor
spread when you know it's not true, even if you aren't
actively saying it. All that kind of stuff. It's telling us not
to lie.

Read Matthew 7:33–37 to find out more about keeping
your word.

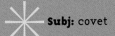
> **Posted by:** JesusInMe
> What does "You shall not covet anything of your neighbor"
> mean?

Dear JesusInMe,

That means you aren't supposed to sit around all day
thinking about what other people have, wishing you could
have it. In the American Heritage Dictionary it says to
covet is to "wish for excessively and longingly." What
happens is you start feeling bad that you don't have what
others have. You think what God has given you isn't
enough and your life would be so much better if you could
only have this or that. God wants us to love what He's given
us and to get over all the other stuff in the world that *could*
be ours but isn't.

Check out more in Matthew 7:7-11.

Dear JesusFreak,

When God created the world, He did it in 6 days and then He rested. He knows that for humans it is very important to have a time of rest and to have a time of worship. So when He gave Moses the 10 Commandments one of them was just for that. God wants us to take at least one day a week and set it aside for Him. He's not just talking about church. He's talking about taking an entire day and dedicating it to Him. In the Old Testament, the Israelites were commanded not to do a thing on that day but love God. They couldn't cook or work, they couldn't go to a movie, or climb a mountain. It was God's day and they were commanded to keep it holy. Though many Christians fail to follow this commandment, it is still a command of God and we should obey it as we obey all the other commandments.

Read Matthew 12:1–6 for more.

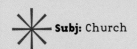

Subj: Church

Dear FED UP,

I don't know if there even is such a thing as a non-messed up church. You know why? Cuz it is made up of humans and we are all messed up. Every church you go to will have some kind of problem or other, that's human. But the one thing that is completely messed up and not acceptable is if they don't believe that the Bible is the inspired Word of God, and that Jesus is our only way to salvation. These are the kinds of churches to stay away from.

Read Revelation 2:1–3:22 to find out more.

Posted by: Ronda

In the Bible God tells us not to be jealous because it is a sin, but at the same time the Bible says that God is a very jealous God. How can this be??

Dear Ronda,

When humans are jealous, it is sinful because it is out of rivalry, envy, competition, or anger. We covet what sinners have and get to do. We are sinful. But with God His jealousy is righteous. In most instances God's jealousy, means "provoked to anger," or "to be zealous." His holiness does not tolerate competing idols or gods, or sin. He's protective in his jealousy, not envious or covetous. In no single passage in the Old Testament is God described as envious. There is no negative connotation to jealousy when it is used with God.

The only instance when humans can be jealous is when they are jealous for their God.

Check out 1 Kings 19:10 and Num 25:13.

Posted by: A girl
Having sex at a young age, is it bad?????? Will God still accept you???

Dear Girl,

God will always accept you, but that isn't the real question. The real question is, do you love God? When people love someone, they want to do things to please them. Having sex when you are young and unmarried doesn't please Him. So for those of us who love Him, we do all we can to please Him, knowing that in that He will take pleasure in us and love and protect us. That's a good thing. Keep it pure. It's well worth the waiting.

You wanna check out more stuff about sex in the Bible? Go to Ephesians 5:3–4; 1 Tim. 5:22; 1 Corin. 6:14–19.

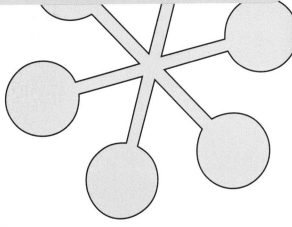

Subj: mythology, against the lord?

Posted by: child of Christ
I wonder if mythology is against the Lord? please reply
when you read this message because i am not so sure.

Dear Child of Christ,

A myth is a traditional story reflecting the beliefs of a
people. The Romans and Greeks used myths to tell stories
about their gods. They were like their Bible. By reading
these, we can learn a lot about their culture and their
beliefs. And we can even learn some things about our own
beliefs and how they differ.

Technically, Jesus also used myths when he preached.
We call them parables. He used stories to explain his
worldview to the people of his time.

There is nothing sinful about mythology as long as it is
taken in context, as with most things; it needs to be seen
for what it is—a story—and enjoyed as such (not idolized).

Read some of Jesus' parables: Luke 8:4–15; Luke 10:25–37;
Luke 13:6–9.

Posted by: Maddogzz
Should cloning be allowed?

Dear Maddogzz,

Cloning is a pretty sticky situation. The first animal cloned was Dolly, a sheep. This was a pretty celebrated event in the world of science. It marked man's achievements like never before.

When Dolly was cloned, however, it brought up the possibility of cloning people. I personally believe that this is unethical. This is man trying to be God. Man is deciding when to bring life into the world and when to make it leave. This is clearly God's job.

Check out these verses about the value of life and God's role in that: Psalm 127:3; Psalm 139:13–16; Jeremiah 1:5; Genesis 11:1–9.

Posted by: Kodie
What do I do if my parents only let me use KJV? I've talked to them about it, but they say the modern versions aren't accurate.

Dear Kodie,
Grab a couple of different versions of the Bible and sit down with your parents. In the front of any translation, it should explain to you how the translation was written. In most any modern translation—like NKJV, NCV, NIV, etc. the scholars who wrote them did extensive research in the original languages to complete the text. They are very accurate. Some versions offer a translation that captures the intent of what the original languages said, sentence by sentence. Others, like the NAS, are word for word translations of the original texts. These may come across as a bit harder to read. Paraphrases of the Bible, like The Living Bible, are not taken from the original languages, but are still very good supplements to your Bible study. I personally think it's very restricting on your Bible Study to use only one translation, no matter what it is. But the thing here is that you have to honor your parents. So sit and talk with them, explain to them that you'd like to deepen your Bible study and see what they say.

"Honor your father and your mother . . ." (Exodus 20:12a).

Subj: i want to be more closer to the Lord

Posted by: Lauren Ashley

I really want to be more closer to the Lord!!!! I know I have to read the Bible and everything and pray but I also want something more!!! I want to feel him reach down on me!!! and talk to me!!!

Dear Lauren Ashley,

What you're looking for is an emotional relationship with God. Sometimes we feel him really intensely. It's like he's right there with us, touching us like you said. But sometimes, we don't feel him. It's like we don't even know he's there.

What you need to do is stay immersed in the Scripture and keep praying your heart out. Eventually, you will be at a point where you can feel him again. But until then, understand that those desert times where you can't feel him don't mean you aren't close to him. He's just taking you on a different path for a while.

Don't base your relationship with God on your emotions. You've got to base it on what you know to be true: Him.

"The heart is deceitful above all things" (Jeremiah 17:9).

Posted by: Anita

My crush likes me back! I am thrilled with it and everything, but his sister kind of has a problem with it. She has been saying things about it behind my back, and the thing about it is, we're supposed to be friends. I also think that she likes my brother, which might be the reason why she seems to be upset or jealous or whatever. I would like to know a godly way to approach her or someone about this.

Dear Anita,

Time to make a decision. Friend or Crush. Your two options. Choose the crush and you will lose a friend forever for a crush that won't last very long. There is no other alternative. These kinds of things can't be fixed by talking it out. So make your choice, but choose wisely.

Posted by: Felicity

I have a problem. We recently moved to a new town. My friends I made there were sassy, dirty talking, gossipy, and mean to people. They stayed inside a little "bad" group. I didn't know until I got moved to the other class. They were totally not the people I wanted to be hanging with. Now they're hangin' all over me and saying stuff about me. They won't leave me alone. I keep trying to ignore them hoping they will buzz off, but they keep getting mad and then trying to get all "buddy-buddy" with me. Can you help me find a way to tell them that I don't won't to hang around people like that? I want to do this in a nice godly way.

Dear Felicity,

What you need to do is find one or two really close, solid Christian friends. They need to be your best friends. They will be the people you can tell anything to, cuz they will look at it from God's perspective. Once you get these friends into your life you just need to make plans with them over these other people.

But, really important, don't write off these other friends. God may be putting them in your life so you can share his grace and love with them. From what you've written, it sounds like they need it.

"Live a life of love just as Christ loved us and gave himself for us" (Ephesians 5:2).

96   Ask **Hayley**

Posted by: Brianna_Banana
I am trying to decide whether I should go to Christian high school or not. If anyone has any pros or cons for me, please let me know!!!!!

Dear Brianna_Banana,

Where to go to high school is a really big decision. Some pros for a Christian high school are that it is often easier to find Christian friends to be a support, and you often have teachers who are educated in the Christian faith teaching you. You can learn a lot more about your faith in an academic sense.

However, a public high school can be a great place to challenge yourself in your faith. You have to be a little bit more bold about it. It might be harder to find Christian friends, but you also get a better perspective of how God's love needs to be shown in the world. Being in a Christian high school can be kinda like living in a cave if you're not careful. You've got a lot more opportunities to witness in a public school.

Why don't you make a list of your pros and cons for each school. It might help you get a better perspective of what you really value, and will help you make your decision.